Doc,
Thanks!

FALLING

FROM

DELAWARE

ISBN 0-9701342-4-X

First Printing

Point Net Publishing
102 Division St.
Petoskey, MI 49770

All names and characters in this book are products of the author's imagination. Any resemblance to any person, living or dead, is entirely coincidental. This book was printed in an environmentally conscious manner by using paper from free-range trees.

CHAPTER ONE

Tonight I'll sit here till the sun comes up or until I die—whichever comes first. Pictures on the wall scoff at me as I wrestle with my failures—photos of relatives, friends, even pictures of myself. They all burn through my soul with judgmental glares, and they are right to do so. I am not the man I used to be. I'm not even a shadow of that person. That Carl Morgan was a reliable, caring, responsible, hardworking... I can't go on, I can only look at the little boy in the picture—the smiling ten-year-old squatting down, petting his dog—and know that I'll never see such purity again in my lifetime.

My stare shifts to a photo of Julia nestled between our parents. I remember that evening so well. We had went down to our cottage for a three-day weekend. It sat up behind the dunes, about two-hundred yards from the sea, right where the Delaware Bay turns into the Atlantic. Julia was eleven and I was thirteen. About a tenth of a mile down from us was another cottage; they had a daughter my age. She was the sweetest thing I'd ever seen. She was there when the picture of Julia was taken. Even though I remember her face vividly, I can't seem to recall her name.

I'd been walking along the beach earlier that day when I

came upon her. I'd seen her from a distance many times before, admired her, longed to see and talk to her, but this was the first time we'd been face to face. We met and she said hello. I asked if she wanted to walk with me—she did—and we began to talk; first about the ocean, then the environment and the recently established Earth Day, and finally ourselves. She was a pleasant, gentle creature with soft, brunette hair that she wore to her shoulders. Her brown eyes had a comforting effect as I found myself passionately discussing things that, until then, I didn't know I cared about. And I recall one thing that happened along the way that I still consider a defining moment in my youth. We passed another kid, a slightly retarded blonde-haired boy. He looked at us, then shied away from the girl and focused on me, and in a deep, awkward voice, said, "Hey man, how's the groove?" He tried to shield his shortcomings with the phraseology of the time, but it was in vain—he was the epitome of social malfunction. So many other times I would have made fun of someone like him, but this time I didn't. I said hello and asked him how it was going. As the girl and I continued down the beach, I fought off the nagging urge to ridicule him, not because I thought she might think it cruel, but because, for the first time in my life, I felt a sensitivity for someone less fortunate; I simply didn't want to do it. I felt good for feeling that way. This girl's mere presence had inspired me to be something better than I was. We walked to the point and sat upon a subtle dune and talked, as a small stream below us emptied itself into the sea. I wanted to kiss her, but I didn't. She was such a unique creature that I didn't want her to think I thought of her as ordinary in any way, for she was unlike any other girl I knew. If I were to have formed an image of feminine perfection, it would have been animated by the girl that I found myself aching for; be it the color of her hair, the purity of her complexion, the shape of her lips, or the inner light that

2

shone through her eyes. We talked until we hit a lull in conversation, then, with both of us fearful of the silence that is so uncomfortable among new acquaintances, we turned and headed back toward our cottages. I told her that we were having a bonfire at dusk and asked if she wanted to come by. She did. I gave her a slight hug, shoulder touching shoulder, and we parted ways and I waited anxiously for evening to fall.

I still remember what she was wearing when she arrived. Unspectacular as it was, it's burned in my memory; a navy sweatshirt that said City College, purplish blue jeans with a white belt of Indian design, and sandals. As she came down the dune I got up to meet her, then led her to my parents and Julia and introduced her to them. My mom asked her if she wanted a s'more. She didn't know what they were but she tried one anyway, and we sat down together on the love-chair swing. Julia came up to us with her camera and took a picture, then asked if I'd take one of her with Mom and Dad.

Back to the wall and my stare blurs the picture of Julia into a vague nothingness and my recollection fades as well, away from a world that's as accessible as recapturing one's youth is possible. Still, that's all I have now—the past, which seems to be confirmed by the lack of any recent pictures. Sometimes I drift back for hours, taking a break from a reality that only offers an ultimate demise. Not such a bad thing to do, but the heavy bass from a teenager's car passing by reminds me that it's no longer 1971.

I think that perhaps a trip to the cottage is what I need. Mom passed away in ninety-six and Dad in ninety-seven, and now Julia and I share ownership. She has a family now; a girl and a boy. I never had children, which was okay with me—until now that is. Again I think back to the girl at the cottage, the girl that I seem to remember every little nuance about—everything but her name—and I think how wonderful it would have been to

3

see her in the eyes of our children. I realize that it's pointless to think of such things, though, and I get off my chair, walk to the closet and pull out my suitcase. I have to go to Delaware. That's all there is to it. It's the only thing I can do to feel anything, and I don't care how harsh the memories may be. I loved going there as a child and the cottage was a warm and comfortable place. But Dad and Mom are gone, and so are those days of opportunity. Yet, I've spent too much time being apathetic to living and I have to taste something. I flop the suitcase on the bed and begin to fill it with three-days worth of clothing. I go through the house, lock down the windows and shut everything off. Five minutes after I got the urge I'm ready to hit the road.

I head out of town and onto I-95. The traffic catches me off guard. I forgot that it was Memorial Day Weekend. I've been so impervious to life that I wasn't aware of any of my surroundings—just as they don't seem to be aware of me. I live in one world and have no link to the other—the world that, for a reason unbeknownst to me, I choose to only vaguely recall, with any recollections of the past coming only in small portions. I go about twenty miles, then, when I see a roadside cafe, I remember that I haven't eaten in two days, so I pull off the highway and go in for a bite. The waitress comes up to me with a condescending scowl, and I realize that a couple of days have also passed since I've showered. Perhaps the dean was right. He'd released me from my teaching position about fourteen months ago, saying that he and the other faculty members felt that since the incident—and I remember him pausing and isolating the word *incident*—I'd lost touch with reality. I didn't know whose reality they were talking about; the world was perfectly real to me—real cold and bitter at first, but then just really bland.

I realize my unkempt state and I don't look at the waitress

when I order scrambled eggs, toast and coffee. She leaves without the formality of a thank-you. I eat without looking at anyone, the waitress returns and silently places the check on the table and I leave without saying another word.

It's a relief to get in my car and be back on the highway. I don't have to live up to anyone's expectations here, I only have to go where the road leads me. Virginia looks good from the rearview mirror and I'm soon in Maryland. Two hours later I get off I-95 and follow Highway 7, which runs up Chesapeake Bay. I turn off the air and open the drivers-side window, letting the salty, sea air blow in. The scent begins to stir memories as I begin to pass familiar sights. My father used to take 7 whenever we went to the cottage. He hated the interstate—preferred the intimacy of the two-lane over the expedience of the freeway. I was the opposite, until now. Now I'm content to meander my way up the coast. I have no job, no reason to be in a hurry, just as I have no reason to be concerned about my well-being.

As I drive I think about the last time I came up here. It must have been a year or two ago, and I have this vague vision of being with the father of the girl I'd met at the cottage when I was young. He was unusually quiet that day, and I can't really remember why he was with me, or how he could have been, because I don't recall having seen him after my senior year in high school, at which time I attended Maryland and no lomger had time to go to the ocean. Still, I get glimpses of him sitting in the passenger seat, holding a cup of coffee and looking out the window as I drove, looking at the poultry farms that lined the rural portion of our route, neither of us saying a word. But it's just a blur to me now—fact or fiction, it's something I refuse to think about. All I remember is the day seemed to go on forever. Those who insist that I've lost touch with reality point to that time period. Those are the people who used to be my friends. They don't stop by or call anymore unless they want to preach to me. How can they tell me how to live my life? I remember the one time I did acquiesce, and that was only because it was Julia who asked me to see this Dr. Reardon. He was supposed to be a topnotch psychologist—a highly educated man of letters. All he said was that I needed to get in touch with my past. I needed to come to terms with everything, then realize what the world can offer me. I've since taken his advice—I realize that the world is dreary and without cheer.

I get to the end of Chesapeake Bay and jump back on the interstate and soon I'm in Delaware. I catch Highway 1 and begin to head south. A couple of hours pass and I'm getting close to the cottage. I look down at the gas gauge and it's close to empty, so I pull into a familiar-looking service station. A man comes out and greets me. "Hey, Carl. It's been a long time. Up for the weekend, hey?" he says as he perches his hands on the car's roof and bends down to my level. He smiles, but his gaze is measuring, just like everyone else's.

I don't remember the fellow, but I answer as though I do. "Yep, up for the weekend. See you're still at the old station."

He nods at me and fills the tank. He smiles as I pay, but says nothing more. Perhaps he doesn't know what to say. I can't blame him, I don't seem to be good at small talk lately. I get back on the highway and figure I have about five miles to go. I turn onto the final road, then after a quarter mile I take the trail of pressed grass which leads to the cottage. I park the car and walk up the weathered, wooden walkway.

The cabin looks the same as it did in 1971, although the brown paint on the siding is beginning to chip. Perhaps that's a good thing. Perhaps I'll stay a little longer than I'd originally planned and fix the place up a bit. A project might be just the thing I need. It'd be good to engage myself in a productive activity again; besides, it'd give me an opportunity to slowly think about life and see if the well is indeed dry, or if there is something left for me. All of a sudden I feel as positive about things as I have in the last year or so, which isn't very positive by most peoples measures, but it's a sign of hope for me. I fumble through my key chain until I find the one for the door. Fortunately I had the cottage key along with my car keys; otherwise I would've forgotten it at home. I enter through the back, go in and put a match to the first gaslight that I come upon, then make my way to the front window and look out toward the ocean. After a minute I take a quick look around to inspect the place. Everything looks in order downstairs, but I'm thirsty and I don't have any fresh water, and I never did care for the water at the cottage. I have to go into town to get paint anyway, so I decide that I'll get a few bottles of Evian when I go. I find a pen and paper as I realize that I may as well make a list of the things I'll need for the next few days. All of a sudden I feel productive, and I don't dread going out in public and facing people. It's been some time since I've felt that way and I'm glad I made this excursion.

Before heading to town I go upstairs. There are no walls in the upper loft, just an open flat with four beds spaced in proportion to where rooms would be. The scent is a combination of pine and stagnant, warm air. I can do without the latter, so I open a few windows and let the May breeze flow through. I see one of the large pines is rubbing against the cottage, which gives me another chore. I look over toward the bed I used to sleep in, the one across from Julia's and on the other side of the stairs from where Mom and Dad slept. I think about how excited I would be whenever we would come here, and how novel it was to wake up to surroundings different than the ones in our Virginia home. I head downstairs, lock up and walk to the car.

I drive into North Shores and pull up to the market, but see that the bank sign indicates that it's eighty-seven degrees, even though it's now twilight. I realize that I should take care of my other business first before picking up refrigerated items. Then when I look at my watch, I figure that the hardware stores are closed and I don't want to get cheap paint at a department store, so I pull back into the market. The paint and supplies will have to wait till tomorrow. I park and walk to the entrance, but when I see my reflection, I remember that I still haven't showered. I feel embarrassed and decide to put off shopping until I come back for the paint, and I get in the car and drive away. And just like that I feel scattered again. Dr. Reardon was right. I'm not thinking clearly. I take a breath and realize that being harsh on myself isn't what I need right now. After all, coming out here was a step in the right direction, even though I'm not sure what direction is right. At least I'm being proactive. I need to look at things from a problematic perspective, but I can't force the issue. I have to let the answers come to me as they will.

I get back to the cottage and begin to remedy the personal hygiene situation. I light the pilot on the hot-water heater, then turn on the faucets to drain the tank of the year-long-standing water. As it's running I take a walk to the beach. The sun is setting and the sight is beautiful, and I realize that I am again enjoying something. I feel the kindling of hope, but as I turn to leave, I look to my right and see the roof of the cottage next to ours peeking over the dune. It's the cottage where the girl from my youth lived, but my uncle, Austin Roarke, owns it now. I stare at it for an indefinite period of time, not quite knowing what I want to do. Then I slowly walk up the dune. Reaching the top I see someone sitting in a lawn chair. It's Uncle Austin. He sees me and waves. I wave back and slowly walk toward him, thinking of what I should say as I approach. He stands to greet me. "Carl, you're looking good," he says as he shakes my hand. I feel relieved that he hasn't broke down in tears like he did last time, but I'm still not sure that I won't. He motions toward a chair and I sit next to him.

"How are you, Uncle Austin?" I ask.

"Oh hell, Carl, I'm about as good as an old man can be. And whenever I get up to the ocean that's pretty damn good. You know, when Gertrude passed away I refused to come back here. It took a long time for things to get back to normal, but time takes care of everything and I sure enjoy being back at this old place again."

I give a sympathetic smile. I know he's saying this for my benefit. He had a long life with someone he cared dearly about and this is his way of telling me to just hang in there and eventually I'll find someone and things will be okay, and looking at him makes me realize that it's possible. Yet, practicality sets in and reminds me that I will be always alone, and that's something I dread. Austin has perhaps ten years to live on his own. I have... well I don't know how long I have. If you measure it by the average life expectancy it's far too long, but if you measure it by the ivory-handled Colt 45 that's in the closet of my Virginia home—the one I'd chosen to ignore at least temporarily before deciding to come to the ocean—then my time alone would be considerably shorter. I look up and notice my uncle staring at me inquisitively.

"You seem to be deep in thought, son, and I don't believe you've heard a word I said."

"I'm sorry, Uncle, I couldn't help drifting."

"I asked how long you'd be up for. Then when you didn't respond, I asked you again."

I look back toward the sea. "I remember the day that I met a girl right over there," I say as I point. "She was walking down the beach... oh, I'm sure you've heard the story many times." I turn back to him. He was choking up, but I said, "I don't know why, we didn't know each other for very long and I barely

9

remember her, but I miss her Austin."

He reaches over and pats my hand in a fatherly manner. "Tell me how long you're staying and I'll go check on you from time to time," he says.

I appreciate his concern and tell him that I'll be up indefinitely. I tell him of my plans to paint the siding, then say that I'll see him tomorrow. I get back to the cottage and hear running water. I'd forgotten that I was flushing the tank and I shut the faucet. I'll have to wait an hour now before I can draw any hot water, so I go out to the car, bring in my luggage and began to unpack. As I do this I regret not bringing more clothes with me, and fresh sheets, too. The ones on the bed smell of must. I add a trip to the laundromat to my list of things to do tomorrow. I should phone Julia as well. I need this time to myself, and as much as I cherish seeing her, I want to make sure that she doesn't have plans to come out for the next week or two.

I sit at the kitchen table until the water is hot, then take my long-overdo shower. It feels good to soak, and by the time I get out it's ten-thirty and I'm ready for bed. I lay on my back and stare up at the pine-board ceiling, feeling insecure and thinking about what Dr. Reardon said to me. I close my eyes and drift back to the times when Mom and Dad would take us out here. It was such an occasion that we'd look forward to it for weeks ahead of time. I wish that I could feel such eager anticipation again.

CHAPTER TWO

We continued to go to the cottage several times a summer, and each time I hoped to see the enchanting girl, but three years passed and our visits to Delaware never coincided. During those times there, I would wake up every morning, hurriedly dress, and rush to the top of the dune that separated their cottage from ours, hoping to see a sign of occupancy. And for the two prior summers that vista had greeted me with crushing disappointment, whereupon I would walk down the beach to the point, following the path the girl and I had taken, before retreating to our cottage with nothing inside me but the anticipation of the next day. It wasn't until 1974 that I'd experience the elation that I had yearned for. Reaching the top of my dune-mountain, I looked toward her place, no longer having expectations, and to my rapture, I finally saw her. Even from a hundred yards away I could see the metamorphosis. She was no longer the cute girl that I'd wanted to be the recipient of my first kiss, but rather a beautiful sixteen-year-old with shapely hips and breasts that left me longing for just a touch. And with that first distant glimpse, my infatuation with her had matured.

I remember the apprehension I felt as I crossed over the dune and approached her. After 1971, we'd kept in touch via letters and phone calls for a couple of months. Then, without being able to see each other face to face, the distance took its toll and my memory was blurred by hometown girls. Still, despite dating several of them and ultimately losing my virginity, the girl at the cottage remained in the back of my mind, and she was unquestionably the best thing I'd ever seen. So, as I went toward their cottage, with her not yet aware of my presence, I wondered what her life had been like, if she had a boyfriend, and I even wondered if she would remember me.

She did.

She turned, having heard my tennis shoes squeak in the dry sand, and with her mouth agape, said, "Oh my God! Carl!" and she wrapped her arms around me, as I did too, as I pressed this new body of hers as close to me as I possibly could without seeming like a pervert. I could feel her boobs against my body and I wanted to grab them. I released and we took a step back and looked at each other. Her face had matured as well; she was no longer a teenybopper, but a young woman. I said her name as she stood there smiling. Ironically, as I was noticing the changes in her, she said, "I can't believe how different you look." My face must have showed uncertainty, because she added, "I mean, you look great."

I guess I hadn't thought of it, but I'd probably changed more than she had. I was about 5'11", seven inches taller than I was in '71, and my body as well, had filled out from its boyish state. I had grown my hair out to a level where it was below my ears and slightly in my eyes, matching the popular style of the early to mid-seventies.

I asked her what she'd been up to, and we spent the next half-hour detailing what'd been happening since we'd seen each other last. Her dad heard us talking and came out to say hello. He was a kind, mellow man and he seemed to like me, and I liked him as well. I asked how long they'd be staying, looking toward him to be conversationally inclusive, and I thanked God when I heard him say three weeks. He went back inside, and the girl and I made plans to get together that evening.

We spent most of that three weeks with one another, and my mother began to refer to her children as Julia and her long-lost son. I had gotten my driver's license and we would head into North Shores every afternoon. It was good to get away from our parents and be free to do as we pleased. We grew fond of a cafe in the center of town. We'd order a little something, then sit for an hour or two and talk. She'd do most of the talking, and I would listen to the soft purity of her voice and admire her beauty. To say that we'd picked up our relationship where we'd left off would be an understatement. The fact was that we were now dealing with adolescent hormones and we were both hot for each other and neither of us tried much to hide it. I remember the first time we kissed. It was getting late and we had promised our parents that we'd be back by dinner. We were heading back to the car after exploring the municipal beach, walking close to one another, and my hand brushed against hers. I felt warmed by such simple contact, and when our arms swung with the next step I caught her hand and held on. She turned to me and smiled—we both knew what we wanted—and I took her, held her face with both hands and kissed her lips. My head rushed as I couldn't believe that something so good was happening. We kissed again, then she gently pushed me back and said, "We have to get back, Carl." I smiled and said that I knew, kissed her again, then took her hand and led her to the car. We were quiet on the ride home and both of us wore foolish smiles. I had fallen for her long ago, and now, she was falling for me, too.

We pulled up to our cottage and decided that we wouldn't try to hide anything from anyone. They could see it in our eyes anyway. I got out of the car, went around and opened her door, and we walked hand-in-hand into the kitchen. My mom was so nonchalant when she noticed us—as if she knew it would eventually happen. She simply smiled and asked her if she'd like to stay for supper. She did.

After we ate, I grabbed my guitar and we walked down to the smoldering bonfire pit. I threw several small chunks of driftwood atop the cinders and as the fire came back to life, I sang, *Dear Prudence, won't you come out to play?* She smiled softly and I kissed her again. We stayed at the fire pit until ten-thirty, singing songs and making out. Then I walked her back to her cottage.

Again I think it strange that I remember that encounter so vividly, yet I can't think of her name. I realize that I've been thinking of her almost nonstop since I've come up here. I recall a conversation that we had the following week. We were tanning at the ocean and talking about summering at our respective cottages, and how fortunate we were to be able to live that way. The dialogue evolved—first to the people we knew that didn't have a vacation home, then to those who we'd see in school that couldn't afford to dress as well as the others, and finally, to the people in the third-world who weren't afforded what we consider to be the most basic of necessities. Somewhere in there we made a pact; we agreed that we'd join the Peace Corps after we finished high school and make our contribution to the less fortunate of the world. It was then, as I looked into her eyes and saw the caring, that I first realized how strongly I felt about her. We made love for the first time that night on a blanket under the stars, protected from the outside world by the dunes that surrounded us. Even though I'd had sex with one other girl, I had never made love before, nor did I know that anything could feel so pure. I wanted to stay with her all night. I never again wanted to get up from that blanket.

I was so inspired back then. I was excited to live my life

and I looked forward to everything that awaited me. Now, I fear social interaction and must force myself to do the simplest of tasks. I sit on the step in back of the cottage and look into the woods, wondering what it was that changed me from such a free, life-loving individual to what I've become now. I know that it wasn't a gradual change. I remember being a socialite as recently as two or three years ago, and I try to remember the point where I became leery of being around others. I get tired of thinking and go back inside.

I focus on the day ahead and grab my shopping list. I add a stop at the clothing store to my agenda. I had packed for three days, but I've decided to stay here for a couple of weeks. I write socks, a couple pairs of work pants, three shirts and underwear on the list, then go upstairs to strip my bed. I bundle the sheets and throw them in the car. I go back inside and plug the refrigerator in and close the door that had been propped open since Julia had last used it. I take a breath and a final look around, then head for town.

I get into North Shores and it's more alive than the previous night. There's an arts and crafts show in the park and streams of people flow past the various stands and displays. I spot the Laundromat that Mom used to go to and I take the sheets in, hand them to the attendant and tell her that I'll be back in a hour and a half. She is a burly old woman and she doesn't seem to like me. I feel relieved—there will be no small talk that way. I leave the laundry and go to the hardware store, where I'm not so lucky. "Carl Morgan," the gray-haired man says with a smile, but he's giving me the same exploratory look as the gas-station attendant. "Up for the holiday weekend?" I think how I not only get the same look from everyone, but the same question, and how everybody in this town seems to be old, and how they remember me but I don't recognize any of them. I tell the gray-haired man that I'm thinking about fixing up the cottage a little and that I'll be up for a while, then ask to see what shades of brown paint they have. He continues his loquacious ways until I pick the color and he goes in back to mix it. I browse around and pick up a couple of paintbrushes, a roller and several pads. Before I leave he looks like he wants to ask me something, but he only nods. I go to the clothing store.

I look through the racks, avoiding eye contact with a sales woman who is looking my way. Peripherally, I see her coming and move to a different rack, hoping she'll know that she isn't needed. She comes to me anyway. "Is there something I can help you find, Carl?" she asks. The fact that she called me by name prompts me to look at her, and this time the face looks familiar. Before I could answer her question she smiles and says, "I remember when your mother would bring you in here when you were a boy, and you were such a fine looking boy," she adds, placing emphasis on the word were. *I was a fine looking boy, but I've grow to be otherwise,* is what I think she's implying, then I remember what Dr. Reardon told me about negativity and I save that inner battle for later. However, the woman seems warm, and the fact that I remember her face from the early seventies makes me feel as though my mother is around the corner looking for a new dress.

"I need some pants—something I can work in," I say. I tell her my size and she takes me to them. They're brown so they won't look too bad if they get paint-stained, and they're reasonably priced, so I buy three pair. I get the others items that I need, thank the woman and head to the grocery store.

The lines at the checkout are long as I walk in and I'm tempted to walk back out, but I need the things on my list and I've already put this off once, so I grab a cart and walk down the main aisle. I manage to avoid conversation this time and I make it through the checkout without having a panic attack. I realize, though, how much of a hassle life has become and I feel anxious to get back to the cottage. I go back to the Laundromat and find that my sheets won't be dry for another fifteen minutes. I go outside and stand at the side of the building and gaze at the people browsing through the art fair. I look to the far end of the park and see an old building which has recently been painted blue. The neon sign says **NORTH SHORE DINER**, and my thoughts go back to the girl and sitting in there as the jukebox played Dylan's *Like a Rolling Stone*. I want to go in, but the last thing I need is to be around more people. However, I talk myself into slipping up to the counter and having a cup of coffee and giving myself the chance to put color to my memories.

The setting looks so familiar for a place that I haven't visited in thirty years. The waitresses are occupied with a line of people waiting for tables, so I feel ambiguous and strangely comfortable. Finally, a rather homely girl in her mid-thirties approaches me and I order a coffee with cream. I look around the joint and spot the turn-of-the-century photos, and I recall having studied the faces in these pictures when I was young. I shoot a glance at the booth that the girl and I would take, drinking it in for a few seconds before an elderly gentleman notices me staring. I take a few minutes before finishing my coffee and leaving, realizing that I'll come back to the cafe again.

I walk back through the park and pick up my sheets. Finally I have everything and I head for the isolation of the cottage. I feel safe there, and as I comprehend this I realize that it's the first time in many months that I've felt safe anywhere. There's a tool shed that stands alone behind the cottage and I carry the painting supplies over to it. I see a figure coming down the grassy path that comes from behind the dunes and connects several nearby cottages to ours. I squint until I see that it's Uncle Austin. I walk toward him and we meet by my car. "Another beautiful day, lad," he says. He smiles and looks

17

out over the sea. I give him a pat on the back and reach into the car and grab the bag full of perishables. He follows me into the cottage. I feel close to this man; he seems fatherly in many ways. As I put everything in the refrigerator, I suddenly can't remember if he was my Mom's brother or my Dad's, or if his wife was the one to whom I was related to by blood. Not remembering this makes me feel fucked up again and I begin to panic. I stand up quickly and grab the cupboards.

"Are you okay, Carl?" he asks with concern, but without overreacting.

"Yes... it's just that I haven't eaten since lunch yesterday and I feel a little lightheaded," I lie. Well, half-lie. It's true that I haven't eaten since then, but I wasn't about to tell him that I panicked because my inability to recall exactly who he was triggered an awareness of just how unaware I am about so many things.

"Come sit down," he says as he takes me by one arm and guides my to the table. "I see some eggs and sausage here. You relax and I'll fix you something."

I'm not hungry for breakfast food, but with what I told him I don't see any other choice than to agree. I look at the happy little gray-haired man with his gentle face and easy manner and I begin to settle down a bit. I reach to a magazine that's on the table and slide it toward me. I start to browse through it and in seemingly no time I have a plate of food in front of me and Austin has joined me at the table.

"Don't you want to eat?" I ask him.

"No thanks, Carl, I've already eaten." He pulls the magazine toward him in what-you-got-there fashion, then slides it back and asks, "Are you starting your project today?"

I nod yes, finish chewing and say, "I picked up everything this morning and I'll start painting as soon as I finish eating and change clothes."

"You can't paint yet, Carl. You've got to scrape it down first or it'll all chip away again."

I realize he's right and I nod, and I realize that I should have known that. Again, I begin to feel incapable of doing the simplest of tasks without someone governing me and again I feel insecure, and suddenly I want this kind old fellow to leave. "There's a scraper in the shed," I tell him, and without thinking of a diplomatic way to say it, I add, "but I feel the need to be alone now."

"I understand," he says with gentlemanly graciousness, and stands up and tells me, "I'll come back and check on you this afternoon." I tell him thanks and he leaves. I wonder why he would feel the need to come check on me. I'm an adult and I wouldn't think it normal for one adult to be compelled to check on another. Not that he isn't right. I just didn't realize that my problems were so apparent. My stock in Dr. Reardon rises.

I get the ladder out, lean it against the cottage and begin to scrape. The sun is out and it's a beautiful day and my outlook improves. I scrape away at the top log and go as far as I can reach, then look off into the grassy dunes that roll softly behind the shed and out to a small patch of birch trees that end the beach and begin a wooded area that leads to the main road. Birds chirp gleefully in symmetry with the May splendor and I allow my mind to at least contemplate entertaining myself when my work day is completed. I climb down the ladder and move it over several feet, scrape what I can reach, then again let myself drift before moving the ladder. I think about building a bonfire on the beach—like we used to do when Mom and Dad were around—and inviting Uncle Austin for s'mores. With the next move of the ladder I go inside and look for the transistor radio. I find it, but the batteries had been left in it and the chamber is badly corroded. I throw the batteries away and clean out the compartment, then take ones out of the flashlight. I turn it on and it works, so I bring it out and turn the dial till I find something that doesn't annoy me. Then I go back to my task. Uncle Austin shows up about two hours later. I hadn't seen him coming down the path this time and I'm slightly startled as he calls up to me. I come down and take a drink of bottled water that I have on the back step.

"Off to a good start, Carl. It's looking good," he says as he checks my work.

I've felt progressively better as the day has gone along and I'm no longer uneasy about his company. "Yes, it's slow work, but it's a start," I respond. The gentle breeze from early morning has stiffened and the air is not as thick as it was the day before. I turn into it and let the wind dry the perspiration off my face.

"Would you like me to fix you a sandwich or something?" Austin asks.

"No, Uncle. I'm still full from breakfast, but would you like to come for a bonfire and s'mores this evening?"

"And we could listen to the baseball game," he adds, seeming pleased that I suggested it. It sounds good to me—like a hint of normalcy. I haven't listened to a baseball game in years, but listening to one would remind me of my youthful days here and how we'd listen to the Washington Senators, and later the Baltimore Orioles after the Senators had moved their team down to Texas. Austin hangs out with me for another fifteen minutes, then returns to his cottage, and I spend the rest of the afternoon scraping. By five o'clock I've finished one side of the building and I figure that it would be an ideal time to leave off and pick it up again the next day. I go inside, take a shower and have a sandwich. I make a quick run into town to get s'more supplies, then settle in for a nap.

I rise at twilight, wash my face and walk outside to inspect my day's work. The air off the ocean is fresh and the evening is warm. I walk around the cottage and decide which side I'll work on next. Off in the distance I hear another neighbor's dogs barking incessantly, but my immediate surroundings are still and quiet. Even the ocean sounds restrained. I walk back inside, gather the marshmallows, graham crackers, chocolate and paper plates and put them into a paper bag, along with some old newspapers that I'll use to start the fire. I grab the transistor radio, then head to the beach and start gathering wood and bringing it to the pit, starting with some small twigs from the birch trees, then some larger branches, and finally some driftwood from the stash that has been collected throughout the years. The driftwood is dry and it will burn fast. It isn't long until Austin arrives, carrying two lawn chairs. He sets them up as I arrange the wood and light the crumbled-up newspapers. The twigs start to crackle and the fire begins encircling the larger branches, ascending to the bottom of the slabs of driftwood. Soon, the bonfire is legitimate. Austin takes a jackknife from his pocket and whittles the bark off one of the twigs, then sticks a marshmallow to it. "How long do you think you'll be staying?" he asks me again.

"Well, I was only planning to stay a few days, but I've found a lot of things to do, so it might be a couple of weeks—or maybe even a month."

He pulls the browned marshmallow off the stick, wedges it between two graham crackers and a slab of chocolate and puts it on a plate, then hands it to me. He reloads his stick and puts it back over the fire, holding it at a distance where it won't catch flame. I take the radio and tune in the Orioles, who are trailing the Red Sox 2-1 in the bottom of the second. The faint sound of the ocean provides an appropriate backdrop for the game and life once again appears to be as it should. Austin slaps a s'more together for himself, and through a mouthful he asks, "How would you feel about a little companion, seeing

21

that you might extend your stay?" I don't know what he's getting at, but before I can ask, he continues. "I was reading the paper yesterday and the animal shelter had a piece about some of the strays that would be put to sleep if somebody didn't adopt them. I felt kind of bad, and I took a ride into town to see what kind of critters they had. There was one dog that caught my eye, would be a good dog for the cottage. I figured I'd get him and he could stay with you until you went back to Virginia. Then I'd take him from there."

I contemplate it briefly, then raise my eyebrows. "Sure, why not?" I tell him. "What kind of dog is it?"

"It's a beagle—cute little bugger. I think he'll keep you good company while you're here."

It did sound kind of interesting to have a little buddy with me. It would probably be good for me as well—to be responsible for something. I take another bite of my s'more. Austin comments as the Red Sox score another run. We run out of things to say and we're both content to listen to the game as we look out toward the ocean.

Morning arrives and I have a quick breakfast followed by finalizing my work assignment for the day. It has cooled off since last evening and for the first time since I came out here I have to put on a sweatshirt. Yet, the temperature is ideal for the work that I'm doing and I set a good pace. Shortly after lunch Uncle Austin pulls up in his Pontiac. He opens his door and out jumps a yellow and white beagle, who immediately darts toward the ocean, then rushes back to the car. He barks a few times, does a lap around the cottage, then stops in front of me. I bend down and give him a couple of strokes on the head and he muffles out another half-bark. "Hey there, boy," I say as I squat down to get a good look at him, then look at Austin and ask, "he is a male, isn't he?"

"Yep," the old man replies. "His name is Tipi."

The dog sits patiently as I pet him, then goes on another run as soon as I stand, only to return back to us. He seems to be a middle-aged dog—old enough to realize his boundaries, but young enough to be sprightly. I say to Austin, "Thanks, Uncle, I can tell I'll enjoy his company." Austin stays for a cup of coffee, and before he leaves he goes to his car and gets some supplies for Tipi from the trunk. I pour the dog a bowl of water, then go back to scraping.

Evening comes and I've finished another side of the building. Tipi has been running around most of the afternoon, exploring his new surroundings, and now lays flat on the hardwood floor in front of the picture window that faces the sea. Austin has yet to check on me since lunch. Perhaps he feels that the little dog and I will keep each other safe.

CHAPTER THREE

Thunderclouds loom in the western sky as I coax myself to slap paint on the cottage, which is more of a labor than it was yesterday. As I do what has become my usual drifting between ladder repositioning, I think of the seventies and the options I had in front of me. I think of what I could have had, what I could have been and what I could have become, and specifically, what my life would have been like had I married the girl of my youth. Now, I stand here alone and paint—a fucked-up, disillusioned recluse serving my self-imposed exile at a cabin that's sole purpose is a setting for me to get my shit together. The gung-ho feeling I had the day before has been compromised by the tedious nature of the job, and I have to force myself to keep from abandoning this project.

Weather reports on the radio have called for a broad band of thunderstorms to come into our area, bringing with it high winds and golf-ball sized hail. I make plans to finish the section I'm working on—a vertical row of five logs which is roughly halfway done—then wrap it up for the day. Tipi's been acting rather strange all morning, not the sprightly little animal he was the day before, and he's waiting for me at the base of the ladder. I climb down and stroke his head, telling him that

I'll be done soon, but he still seems subdued.

The wind has picked up considerably by the time I make my weather-adjusted goal. I put everything away and try to take Tipi for a walk, but he won't go. I squat down and coax him, but a gust of wind sends my Oriole hat rolling and bouncing across the grassy sand, the hat that I'd bought just the other day. I give up on the walk, fetch the hat, and we go into the cottage. I again pat his head, asking him what's wrong in the same voice that one uses to address an infant. He lets out a little sigh and licks my hand, something he hadn't done before. I check his food and water bowls and they're both good. I'm concerned about my little friend, but my answer to his mysterious mood comes as he runs behind the couch with the first nearby lightning strike. The skies darken quickly, leaving a doomsday hue blanketing the earth. I note my dog's intuition and have a feeling that we're in for quite a storm. I light a couple gas lamps, put on a pot of coffee and wait for the deluge to begin.

Another loud crack of thunder marks the beginning of the storm, as the wind pushes heavy sheets of rain toward us at a forty-five degree angle. I watch as it intensifies, and again I think back to the girl of my youth. It was 1975 and the summer before our senior years, and the last time I can remember being with her. The evening was similar to this one, only the day had been hotter and the rain was warm as it touched our skin. We stripped down and ran about the dunes. The girl's rain-soaked hair had grown long enough to touch her breasts, and the beaded raindrops rolled down their suppleness as I knelt to kiss them. The sand was uncomfortably wet and not an option, and I stood and wrapped my arms inside her knees and hoisted her as she held my neck. We stood in the driving rain making driving love, with a passion that releases every nuance of every energy your body and soul have to offer, and as I came she began to cry, and I began to cry along with her. She'd be leaving the next morning and the uncertainty of the future hung over us heavier than the thunderclouds. I lowered her and embraced her tightly, wondering in what direction life would take us, if we'd be able to follow each other, or if this was to be a fiery love affair that was scripted for heartbreak—doomed by the nature of its very being.

I'm brought out of my trance by a loud crash on the roof. Tipi yelps and retreats behind the couch again, and I get up, go to the closet and grab a raincoat. The wind is unbelievably strong as I wrestle to open the door, and once I'm outside I must lean into it to keep my balance. I round the corner of the building and see the huge pine has fallen, with the upper half crashing upon the roof. I try to climb it, as it rests at a favorable angle for doing so, but I'm getting peppered by hail and the tree is slippery and I don't want to fall while I'm here alone. I go back inside and inspect for water damage. It seems darker, so I take the batteries out of the radio and put them back into the flashlight, then go up into the loft. The tree came down in the vicinity of where Julia's bed is, and I shine the light above it. There's a small trickle coming down from the space between the varnished pine boards that make up the ceiling. I drag the bed out of the way and go downstairs to look for a pail. I find one under the kitchen sink, complete with rags and sponges, just the way Mom used to keep it. I go back upstairs and place it under the leak, but the water is beginning to run the span of the pine board and where it will fall is becoming unpredictable. I run out to the shed, fighting off the wind again, and find two five gallon buckets. I arrange them the best I can, realizing that they will have to do, then grab a blanket and pillow and head downstairs and wait out the storm.

After fixing a light dinner I lay on the couch. Tipi jumps up on me and I pull him to my chest. He seems comforted by this.

I wish that I could feel protected so easily. Soon, the sound of the storm placates me and I fall asleep, and by the time I awaken it's eight o'clock and the rain has subsided. I check the upstairs for water damage but it's not too bad; all I'll have to do is wash Julia's bedding and air out her mattress. Tipi and I take a walk to Austin's to see how he had weathered the storm. Everything is okay and we hang out for an hour. Then I return to my cottage and call it an early night. Gathering my blanket and pillow, I head upstairs.

The next day begins the same with Tipi hitting the edge of my mattress until I'm awake. I rub my eyes. "Okay, you little bugger," I say as I sit up and stretch. I go to the window, spread the Venetian blinds and peer through. It's overcast and it looks like it will rain again within several hours; however, it looks warm, so I take Tipi outside without bothering to get dressed. As he runs around, I scan the tree, starting from roots protruding from the uplifted earth, diagonally up the trunk, through the mass of needles and branches and onto the damaged roof. It would have been nice to take a day off, but with another storm on the horizon I know I have to patch things up right away.

After a quick breakfast of scrambled eggs and toast, I dress, get food and water for the dog and rest a ladder against the west end of the building. The west end is the only side where the ground is soft and free of protruding roots. I've developed a slight ear infection, the end result of a summer cold, and it's affecting my balance, so I pick the side with the softest ground for the ladder as a fail-safe. I climb up and look at the sky, trying to judge the time I have before it opens again. I decide that I don't have time to clean up all of the fallen tree—just the part that has torn up my roof, so I fetch a hand saw from the storage shed and cut off branches until the damaged area is clear. When the tree fell, a branch had been broken, leaving a sturdy, short butt that tore through the shingles and tarpaper upon impact. The tear is about a foot and a half long, but fortunately there's no damage to the wood beneath it. I don't believe I have anything to fix it here, and even if there was a can of tar I'm sure it would be dried up, so I run into North Shores. As I go through the lumber yard I hear the locals talking about the storm, and about the one on the way. I get a can of tar, a roll of tarpaper and a putty knife. As I head back out of town I feel an urge to stop at the diner, but I know I can't spare the time; yet it feels good just to have an urge to do something in the presence of people. With the exception of Uncle Austin, I've become something of a hermit, and I know that social interaction is another step toward normalizing my life.

I return to the cottage and bring my supplies up on the roof. I rip off the damaged shingles and cut off the torn tarpaper, then cut another slightly larger piece with which to replace it. I pull back the undamaged shingles and tuck the new piece into place, nail it down, then tar over the seams and nail heads. Then I cover the area with a plastic tarp, putting some old bricks underneath to raise the plastic so it doesn't touch the wet tar, and secure it with rope to the side of the roof, pulling on the rope to make sure it's taut. I can hear thunder in the distance as I put the ladder away, and I feel proud for being self sufficient. I call Tipi and we head down the path to Austin's. The rain begins to fall as we reach his porch. He sees us and comes out.

"Looks like you got here just in time. C'mon Tipi," he says with a whistle as he opens the door. Tipi runs into the cabin and Austin and I sit at the kitchen table that rests near the window—just as at my cottage—and we look out over the ocean as the light rain turns into a downpour. "Would you like a cup of coffee?" he asks, "or perhaps a cup of hot cocoa?"

I opt for the cocoa and he makes a cup for each of us. "I got the roof fixed just in time, Uncle," I tell him as I take a sip.

He smiles. "How is everything else going?" he asks, seemingly disregarding my accomplishment.

"It's going okay," I tell him. "I've been spending a little time in town lately. Been going down to the diner." I want to tell him that I feel comfortable there, but such a statement would further reveal just how fucked up I am. After all, why would a normal person profess with pride that he felt comfortable in a diner? But then again, he does know that things aren't well with me—he checks up on me every day. I begin again to try to understand what's making me feel the way I do. Things were normal not so long ago; that much I remember.

The wind picks up and I'm hoping that the tarp hasn't blown off my roof. Tipi barks at a nearby lightning strike and cowers into a space between the couch and the wall. Austin calls him and the dog comes over and hops onto his lap. Austin looks natural with this animal as he pats it atop the head in fatherly fashion, and the dog lets out a little breath of relief. I see the easygoing nature of my uncle and I long to talk to him about myself, but I can't get up the gumption to speak about such a topic. Instead, we sit quietly and listen to the sound of the storm. An hour passes. The rain is falling even harder and the wind is driving it toward the cabin, causing it to make a spattering sound as it hits the window. A dampness fills the cottage and Austin builds a fire. I realize that the rest of the day will be lost, so I resign myself to an afternoon of conversation and hot cocoa.

As the hours progress, so does the intensity of the downpour. Austin has dug out a game of scrabble and we play until dinner, when he fixes sloppy joes. Afterwards, we resume our gaze, fixated out over the sea, and become redundant in our talk of the storm. I begin to get bored and Tipi is restless, so I think about making a run for it and hopping in the shower when I get back. I'm still curious about how my patch job is holding. I'm about to leave when, in a low, gravely voice, Austin says,

"This reminds me of the times you and Renee would come here." He stares out the window and suddenly looks very lonely. He means Julia, of course, but I don't have the urge to correct the old man and I'm left not knowing what to say.

It's not until six when the storm subsides enough for me to go back to my cottage. The old man looks lonely, so I leave Tipi with him for the night. I run home through what's left of the rain, shake the wet sand off my shoes and leave them at the door. It feels good to be back, and despite the fact that I've become attached to my little dog, it's good to have a night alone.

From that point the days passed swiftly. As the Memorial Day weekend had turned into a month, that month turned into a summer at the cottage. I continued to work on various projects, every day I'd go into town and have lunch at the diner, and in the evening Austin and I would listen to the Orioles at the bonfire. I'm seeing the fruit of my work and feeling better about myself. The Delaware experience has made me a little more grounded than I was when I arrived, but I still feel an uneasiness that I can not explain. Yet, I feel increasingly comfortable at the North Shores Diner. Of everything I've accomplished, being at ease around these people is the feat I'm most proud of, even though they're mostly locals who knew me from the past. I talk normally with them and speak of what I'm doing to fix up the cottage, and the older ones talk about my mom and dad. There's a waitress named Molly that I've befriended. On occasion we walk to the park after her shift and talk. She's new in town, so I have no ghosts with her. She's small framed, slightly underweight, and could be construed as being homely. Her dress is pedestrian, but she has an earthy way about her that makes me feel equal and easy with her.

The more I get to know her the more comfortable I am, and I begin to talk about some of the fears I've had. It feels good to let some of this stuff out with someone other than Dr. Reardon; someone who'll listen while I myself try to make sense of what I'm saying. We begin doing things on her days off. Having explained my phobias to her, she knows my limitations and goes out of her way to accommodate me. We go to movies and sit in the back row, or go for simple walks down some of the country roads. She talks to me about how she'd been in an abusive relationship down in Georgia, and how, after tolerating the mistreatment for eight-plus years, she finally got the nerve to break free and start anew. The fact that she's also somewhat damaged make me feel even more akin with her.

Thursday arrives and brings with it the month of August. I take a minute to get an overview of what I've accomplished, and I'm pleased with the results. I have the siding scraped and painted, my temporary patch on the roof is holding, and I'm in the process of replacing the warped and cracked boards on the wooden walkway that begins at the front door and extends across the sand to the fire pit. I like this chore, as it's an immediate improvement as far as I progress, and never bears that project-half-done look. Tipi has gotten accustomed to me now and is within three feet at any given time. Austin has been tinkering with an old sailboat that he had bought in the eighties as a fixer-upper, but he never got around to doing anything with it until now. I've been keeping myself occupied, but I wonder how I'll be when I run out of things to do and have more time to think.

I wrap up my work at the cottage by three o'clock, hop in the shower and drive into North Shores to pick up Molly. I go to the diner and have a cup of coffee as I wait for her to finish, whereupon I follow her home, sit on the sofa and watch television while she changes out of her work clothes. She comes out of her bedroom and stands in the doorway and asks if I need anything while I'm waiting. I turn to answer and see that she's wearing only her bra and panties. Despite the fact that she doesn't have the most attractive face, her body is quite appealing. I smile and tell her that I'm alright and she goes back into her room. She comes out ten minutes later, dressed and ready, and we get into my car.

We decide to get out of town for the evening and drive down to South Bethany. I'm feeling strange about Molly coming to the doorway in her underwear, and the silence in the car reveals the fact that it's on my mind. Finally, she asks me if I feel uncomfortable. I tell her that I do, then pull to the side of the road. She turns and faces me while I stare straight ahead. "What is it?" she asks.

"I'm not sure," I say. "I enjoy your company and we have a good time together, but there's something I need to figure out before I get involved with someone else. It's hard to explain, but when I looked at you as you came out of the bedroom, it felt as though I was cheating on someone and I felt guilty for the thoughts that were going through my head." I turn and face her. "Does that make any sense to you?"

"Of course not," she says, but she takes my hand and adds, "but it's not me that's in your shoes."

I give her hand a quick squeeze, then pull the car back onto the road. I ask her if she still wants to go to South Bethany and she says she does, and I tell her that I do, too, and we find a mid-priced restaurant and have dinner. It takes a while for the uncomfortable feeling to dissipate, but eventually it does and we get back into our usual conversation. After we eat we take a walk through town and drink in the fresh scenery. Then, I take her home. I give her a kiss on the cheek, thanking her for understanding me, and I head back to the cottage.

As I lay in bed, I try to figure out what had bothered me about the event at Molly's. Though I hadn't previously thought about a physical relationship with her, it would be logical, and being with her would be a positive for me. I get frustrated and wonder why I'm so different than what I used to be.

I continue to see Molly several times a week as the final days of the summer pass swiftly. We maintain friends status, and probably enjoy each other's company more than before our uncomfortable incident. I continue to find projects at the cottage and I feel proud of what I've been able to achieve over the course of the summer.

With Labor Day weekend only a few days away, I begin making plans to return to Virginia. I'll hate to leave the cottage, but I have already phoned Julia and told her that she and her family could have it for the holiday. After all, I have hogged it for the entire summer, and I have to return to home eventually. Still, I feel now that this is more my home than my house in Virginia. I decide I'll stay three more days, then leave on the Thursday before the holiday weekend. I didn't bring much with me so packing will be easy, and the extra work clothes I bought I'll leave here for the next time I take on a project. I have my usual small breakfast, then head down the path with Tipi to Uncle Austin's cottage.

I knock on the door but there's no answer, so I walk to the beach as Tipi runs in circles around the path I'm taking. I hear an "Ahoy," as I come over the last dune and see the white-haired head of my uncle pop out of the boathouse. Tipi sees him and goes into a sprint as Austin crouches down to meet him. I catch up to the dog and Austin shakes my hand, then shows me the work he's been doing on an old boat that hasn't sailed for years. The salty smell of the sea awakens my senses as I listen to him talk about how he'd like to get out on the ocean one more time. "But I realize that I'm an old man," he concludes. He seems subdued again today, which isn't his nature. I suggest that we go to his place for a game of scrabble, but he says he isn't up to it. Nonetheless, we head back to his cottage. I sense that he's feeling a little lonely; I can't recall how long it's been since my aunt died, in fact I can't remember her at all. I worry about how he'll be after I leave. He'll be returning to Germantown, Maryland, but not until October, and although he's been the one checking in on me, I wonder how he'll be on his own. I'm sure he realizes that I have to return to Virginia, but I hope he won't take it hard when I tell him that I'm leaving in a few days. Finally, I say, "I have to get back home soon, Uncle."

The old man tightened his ever-so-slight smile into a concerned look. I sense that he's going to take it hard. He clears his throat and I expect him to say something gallant, *I'll be alright,* or *Don't worry about me,* but instead he says, "Carl, it's time you come back to us." He pauses as I furrow my forehead, not having a clue about what he means. He looks at me with intense seriousness and says, "I'm not your Uncle Austin. If you think hard you'll remember. I'm Renee's father."

Something in what he says jolts me and I feel my body begin to tremble. His voice cracks as he continues. "You married Renee in 1979 and you had two children, Daniel and Prudence." His right hand begins to shake and suddenly I can't look at him—I'm used to him being solid—and my mind is racing. I feel like my head is about to explode and everything around me is a whirlwind. He looks at me carefully, as if gauging the effect of his words, then says, "Eighteen months ago today all three of them were killed when the car they were driving collided head-on with another vehicle."

"Shut up!" I scream and I drive at his knees to tackle him, but land with my face in the sand. I spring back up and push the old man and he falls backwards into the sand.

He rubs his head, then cautiously gets back up, keeping his eye on me as he does. "I know you don't want to hear this, Carl," he says as he slowly walks up to me and puts both hands on my shoulders and shakes me, "but you have to! For your own good—you have to hear this!"

But I can't hear another word. That day flashes back to me with lightning impact and I see every vivid moment of it in split-second time: the cop at my door, the car with the front end crushed beyond survivability, the quick glance when identifying the bodies, the company at the house trying to console me, and finally, Julia taking me in to the emergency room, where they sedated me and kept me for the night. All these things flash through my mind, over and over again—Renee—the girl from the cottage whom I loved in my youth. The girl whom I'd gone to the diner with and the girl that I made love to fourteen times during our summers at the ocean—yes—she was my wife! And our two little children! I'm gasping for air and suddenly I see Austin still holding my shoulders and he's crying, and I break away and run. I run back to my cottage, grab my keys and run out to the car. Tipi is frantic and tries to get in, but I push him away, slam the door and drive off with the pedal floored.

CHAPTER FOUR

I storm from the cottage with my little dog chasing me down the road. I feel a thump under the back tire and I don't know if I hit him or a bump, but everything is swirling and I can't distinguish reality from fiction, and everything feels either obscure or surreal. I fly through North Shores, take the first road I come upon and drive for hours before I think about anything. The trees blur past me peripherally as though I'm exceeding 100 MPH. Whether I'm going that fast, I don't know and I don't care. My head is still buzzing—not a descriptive expression—the noise is real. There's no playing of the radio, no stopping at rest areas, no looking for restaurants or hotels; it's straight forward and unmindful driving until I run out of fuel and steer the stalling car off to the shoulder. I get out and look around, and that's the first cognizance I have of what I'm doing. I don't know how long I've been driving, I don't know what route I took that got me to where I am now, I only know that I'm on an unfamiliar and seldom-traveled county road with dawn approaching.

The air is cool and without a jacket and I begin to shiver. I walk up the road, continuing in the direction that I had been heading before my car stalled. I walk for at least an hour before a man comes up behind me in a horse-pulled carriage. "Is that your vehicle back there?" he asks, but I don't answer. I just keep putting one foot in front of the other with no apparent purpose or end result in mind. "Are you a deaf man?" He asks again, not sarcastically but with genuine curiosity. I look up and see an Amish face. Something in his stoic yet unassuming manner relaxes me and, for the first time since I dashed from the cottage, I focus.

I look up at the man, with his long beard and wide-brimmed hat, and ask, "You don't happen to have a can of gas, do you?"

"We don't use gasoline," he says with a sincerity-filled earthy humbleness. He doesn't explain, although I'm sure that I look somewhat dumbfounded. "Come on with me," is all he says. "I'll give you a ride into town."

I call him Abe Lincoln as I climb onto his carriage, where-upon he gives a slight chuckle, tells me that his name is Henry Olafson and asks me for mine. I ask where we are and he says just outside of Mountville—I have to ask the state, and he tells me Pennsylvania. We ride a little further down the road and he points to his farm, which is to our left as we travel, and upon reaching town and seeing everything closed, he takes me back to the farm, telling me I can stay until the gas station opens. I go into his barn and lay on the straw as he begins his workday. Through the sound of him pounding on iron, I doze off and don't wake until I'm rousted by him, telling me he had decided to let me sleep, but that it's supper time now and to come to the table and eat with him and his family.

Still physically drained despite the long nap, I sit up and rub the sleep out of my eyes. I look out the barn door and see my car parked in the grass along the dirt road that leads to the house. I rise and follow Henry into the house and to the dinner table. I sit, and a woman in a long, plain dress and a white bonnet, whom he introduces as his wife, Sarah, places a bowl of cabbage and beef stew in front of me, along with two hard rolls. Henry sits at the head of the table, and when Sarah has placed everything, she sits at the other end. I'm on one side, and across from me are two little children, a boy and a girl, both of whom were dressed like their parents. Henry doesn't introduce them to me. He bows his head and says grace, then we eat. Things are quiet throughout most of the meal. When we're almost finished, though, Henry dismisses his children, turns to me and says, "You're welcome to stay with us for a while." I look up at him, trying to think of a reason to say no without offending him, but before I can, he adds, "I know what happened to your family."

I don't know what he's talking about.

"Sheriff John is a friend to our community; he looks out for us. When he noticed that your car had sat alongside the road all day, he went to some of the farmhouses to see if anyone knew whom it belonged to. When he got here, I told him that it was yours and that you were sleeping in the barn. He warned me about being over trusting, ran your license plates, then called your hometown sheriff. That's when we learned of your terrible tragedy."

I shrug my shoulders. "I'll be okay," I say as I stuff the last half of my dinner roll into my mouth.

"Your sheriff told us that you were still having a hard time with things; having trouble accepting them."

I start bouncing my knee and suddenly want this bearded stranger to shut up, and perhaps he senses this because he doesn't say anything more about what I'm supposedly going through. "So I'll go back to my original question to you, Mr. Morgan. Would you like to stay here for a while? Harvest time is coming soon and I could use a hand."

I would like to be away from anything familiar, that much I know. But I have a vague memory of having some kind of incident with Uncle Austin, who in turn must have spoken with Julia by now. I don't feel willing or ready speak with either of them, so I answer with a stipulation. "I'll stay and help if you promise not to let my sister or uncle know that I'm here."

He rests his elbows on the table, folds his hands in a thinking man's manner and tells me, "Our religion forbids us from making binding promises, I'll only assure you that you won't have to worry about it. You know, Carl, the culture you'd be submerged in is very pure and basic. It would be ideal for someone who seeks quiet and solitude." He gets up and we walk outside, and he tells me more about the Amish, beginning with how they are simple and self-sufficient and have little interaction with the outside world. He says that they don't use public utilities, but he tells me that he does have a generator that produces his own electricity, and that their water comes from a well. He explains how some of their customary laws have been circumvented, but just enough to do business with the English—the English being their designation for anyone who is not Amish. He tells me that they educate their children in a one-room schoolhouse, and that the youths can experiment with the ways of the outside world until they come of age. At that point they can choose to leave the community if that is their desire, but if they select the traditional life, then they can never go back on that decision.

He says that I'll have to sleep in the barn this evening—and I notice how he refers to the day ending in the evening—but says that he'll have a room in the house ready for me by the next day. I'm sure he'd contact someone if he knew how worried Julia and Austin must be, but he's a simple man who seems to take life at face value, and I sense that I'll benefit from him being that way.

I find out the next morning that getting up when the rooster crows is more than an expression. Henry wakes me, saying that breakfast will be ready in five minutes. I feel re-energized; I've slept well. The rising sun brakes through the trees, leaving patches of reddish-yellow sunlight outside the barn door. I rise and go to the outhouse, then splash water on my face at the pump and make my way to the house. There's a hearty breakfast of eggs, ham, potatoes and hard rolls at my spot. Everyone but Sarah is already seated. As soon as I sit, she asks me if I need anything, and when I tell her that I don't, she sits as well. Henry says grace, then we begin to eat. A light conversation follows, as Henry asks the children what they'll be learning in school. They answer politely, and the little girl shyly smiles at me as she speaks to her father. Sarah sits and listens. She seems friendly for someone who seldom says anything. When we finish eating, Henry leads me back to the barn.

I'm given simple, adolescent-worthy tasks, the first of which is cleaning out the horse stalls. Henry rolls a wheelbarrow over and hands me a shovel and a garden rake. What has to be done needs no explanation, so I take a deep breath and get to it. By the time I finish the second stall I already feel the wholesomeness that Henry had referenced. Through the choking stench, I see the approaching Pennsylvania autumn as an opportunity for me to ground myself, to determine what happened at the cottage that gave a summer of accomplishments such a disastrous ending.

I throw fresh straw into the stalls, then look for Henry for my next task. I find him behind the barn. He's wearing a straw hat today along with bib overhauls, and if one had a preconceived image of an Amish man, he would fit the picture. He tells me to organize the rest of the barn, but as I go in, it looks organized already. I tinker with it though, killing time more than anything, and I allow myself to think about what happened immediately before I left the cottage. I remember going to the boathouse and talking with Uncle Austin, I recall speeding off angrily, and as I think more, I realize that I might have run over Tipi. *What the fuck could have happened that'd make you lose control like that?* I ask myself. I get choked up when I think about the little dog, but the bigger problem, manifested in my trembling hands, is the lack of an answer to a question that I refuse to focus on for more than a couple of minutes.

Henry comes in and has a disappointed look as he sees me sitting on a bale of hay, but as he notices me drying my cheeks with my sleeve, his expression relents and he softly asks me to go to the field with him. He grabs a burlap bag from a bin and I follow him out the door. Tall stalks of corn tower over our heads as I walk behind him. I force myself to let the incident with Austin go so I can concentrate on what Henry assigns me. I want to do a good job for this man. He's a good fellow, and although I'd guess him to be ten years younger than me, I feel that I can learn something from him—not just about farming, but about life. He seems to contain the knowledge of generations of Amish farmers, knowledge accrued from hardship, ridicule and simplicity of means. As we emerge from the corn there lies a small field of assorted vegetables, similar to what one would plant in their backyard. He hands me the bag and says, "We'll be having stew for supper."

Again? I think.

"We'll need some potatoes," he pauses and I can tell he's counting how many we'll need, "eight of them, ten carrots, a celery and a turnip, a head of cabbage, two rutabagas and about three beets." I look perplexed and Henry asks if I got it all, and I tell him that I did, but with some embarrassment I admit that I don't know a rutabaga from a turnip. He points to distinguish the two for me. He tells me to bring them into Sarah when I'm done, then goes on to explain that I'll be doing a lot of odds and ends for a week or so, but once the harvesting starts I'll have a lot to do. He concludes by telling me to get a feel for things during this time—get to know where everything's at. I tell him that I will, and begin picking the vegetables for supper.

In the evening I decide to take a walk down the county road that runs past the house, which eventually becomes my nightly routine. The days pass in similar fashion for the next month, with Henry finding chores for me during the day, some insignificant and some important, and allowing me to have time to myself during the evening. The walks I take bring to me even more solitude than the Amish farm has to offer. The road is seldom traveled; I may only see ten vehicles pass during an hour-long walk. The more time goes by, the more introspective I become, and once again I find myself in the familiar search for answers.

The road becomes more intimate as the days pass, and the walk is something I look forward to from midday on. The worn and crumbling pavement is my friend, partly because anybody can walk down it, and if anybody can, then I must be somebody, and if I'm somebody, than perhaps I'll once again find out who I am. The ditch follows my path, only occasionally interrupted by a span of culvert burrowing under a dirt drive that leads into a field. Long strands of timothy entwine themselves with a barbed wire fence that also accompanies me. The late summer sun has turned the grass to a sun-baked brown. The October breezes refresh and stimulate my mind and I allow myself to think a little more each day.

I begin to remember the traumatic nature of my departure from the cottage, and each day I try to dig further into the matter. Still, there's a memory block that I can't seem to get through concerning what Austin said to me, right before I shoved him to the ground, ran to my car and sped off. Although I can't remember his words, I know that it had to be profound enough to change the way I think about things. Yet, I know that there's an answer that I need to find, and that's more than I knew when I arrived here. Dr. Reardon had told me that this would happen, and that answered questions would turn into empty glasses, perhaps many times, before I came to wholly accept them as truths.

Time continues to pass and I become more and more useful to Henry. Now that his crops are in full harvest, he has set up a roadside stand at the end of the dirt road that leads from his barn to the county road. I gather the produce for him to sell while he tends the stand. Despite him having stoic and stand-offish nature that is quintessential Amish, he seems to sell lots of vegetables. I think that his customers expect that persona and see it as a badge of authenticity. Perhaps that's why he's never asked me to tend the stand. Then again, perhaps it's the common business sense of not wanting a screwed-up individual handling your money. Either way, I prefer being alone in the field and not having to deal with people face to face.

Autumn passes swiftly, and with that, I believe that I'm beginning to regress again. I've failed to have any deeper recollection of what had happened when I fell from Delaware, and although Henry has been keeping me busy with chores that will prepare the farmhouse for a Pennsylvania winter, he has hinted that I'll have to move on when the work has been done. As I think of this, I wonder how I'll be able to cope again on my own. There has been a consistency and security here; everything I need to do has been directed to me by Henry, and everything I need to survive has been provided to me.

The end of my stay comes at the height of my dementia. It's December sixteenth. The first substantial snow of the season is falling, and as the children come home from school, Sarah uncharacteristically goes out to play with them. They're in the yard between the house and the barn, under the large maple tree, and are building a snowman. I watch them frolic and toss snow at each other, laugh and run around the tree as they layer their jolly snowfellow. As I observe, I feel infused with warmth—a feeling of love that I'd long ago forgotten. I go up to them, bend down and embrace the children, one in each arm. "I've missed you so much!" I say to their puzzled faces. Then I stand and take hold of Sarah. "God, I love you!" I attest. I force my lips on hers, following them with my mouth as she tries to turn away. She puts her hands on my waist and tries to push me away. "Renee," I say as I pull her tightly to me. "Everything's going to be okay from now on! We'll move back to Vermont and the kids will be happy, and you and I can be together again. We can buy our old apartment and look out over Lake Champlain at sunsets and..."

I feel a hand on my shoulder as Henry tears me away from his wife. Sarah tells him that everything's under control, but he must have been listening long enough to gather what was happening, for, other than separating me from her, he makes no attempt at further restraint or retribution. He instead gives me a slight tug, the kind that beckons one to follow, which I do, and we go toward the barn. "I don't think it would be good for Sarah or the children if you stayed here one minute longer," he says with no signs of anger or animosity. "We have the clothes that you wore when you came here. They're cleaned and folded. I'll get them and you can get out of these dirty work clothes. You have enough gas in your car to get into town and I have thirty spare dollars for food and gas along your way home."

I nod, and though I don't understand why he's sending me away, the fact that he's telling me to leave occupies all my thoughts. I only have a faint recollection of doing something wrong and thus drawing his ire. He has me wait in the barn as he goes to get my clothes, and stays with me as I change into them. I shake his hand and tell him that I'll go in and say goodbye to everyone, but he holds his hand in front of me. "No, Carl," he says. I don't know why he wouldn't want me to say farewell, but sensing that I've done something wrong, I don't press the issue. He tells me that I need to accept that it was God's will that my wife and children had been taken from me, and I pat his back and calmly say that everything will be okay. I get into my car, and after coaxing it to start, I wave, then turn and drive down the dirt road which leads to the highway.

I drive into town and pull up to the first gas station. Reaching into my pocket, I find the thirty dollars that Henry had promised me. I put ten in the tank and drive down the road, continuing in the direction I'd been heading the night that I met him. The slippery roads occupy my mind and keep me from falling into that mental fog for the rest of the evening, but after pulling over and sleeping in the car, I wake feeling as fucked-up as ever. My head spins as I drive, and my mind rushes with noise that sounds like a stiff wind blowing through a screen. My distorted perception from the day before has unlocked memories of Renee and the kids, which I push down as soon as they come back, but now my doubt of my ability to function is as bad as it has ever been. Mechanically, I get on Interstate 83, wanting to hook up to I-95 and get back to Virginia. Then inexplicably, I exit into Washington D.C., drive toward the heart of the city, fill my tank, then walk away, leaving my car at the gas station as my mind races in symmetry with the sounds of the nighttime streets.

CHAPTER FIVE

I don't understand why I had to leave Henry's farm so abruptly, just as I don't remember what happened to me after I left the cottage in Deleware, but it's winter and I find myself on the streets of Washington D.C. Just when I thought that I'd hit bottom, I've found that I'm able to further sink into the lower echelons of humanity. My mouth is frozen as I walk against a stiff wind, heading for the center of town.

After I had fueled my car the night before, I remember wanting to go for a walk. Leaving the car at the pump, I walked into the icy wind in an attempt to wake up, going several blocks, finding that my car was gone when I returned. After a slight bout of panic, I excused my slip-up and realized that I was in no critical hurry to be anywhere anyway. I didn't feel like dealing with the police, so I decided to walk back through the blocks I had just been down. But the truth was that I really didn't care. I had come to a state of mind that relieved me of all responsibilities. I came to realize in a quite unemotional way that either I'd survive or I wouldn't. As the night progressed it became colder. I walked to keep as warm as I could, but when I was too tired to continue, I curled up on the steps of a business' alley entrance and closed my eyes and didn't move until I heard the sounds of the waking city.

Now my bones hurt from sleeping on the street. I stand, holding my arms close to my body for warmth, and for the first time it hits me that I am officially homeless—homeless and unemployed—and probably a little bit whacked. Perhaps I should have spent more time with Dr. Reardon. Perhaps all of this could have been avoided. I begin to walk toward the center of town.

I've yet to come across anyone in the same predicament as myself, although I know that D.C. does have a rather large community of homeless. The only pedestrian traffic consists of business professionals and shoppers, and I notice the bags of the latter and realize that Christmas is only a short time away. The fact is that I'd totally forgotten about it, just as I seem to be oblivious about so many other things these days. The only thing that I seem to remember is the girl at the cottage, the one that Austin—who was never my uncle—had talked about before I left. I can't remember what he said, but I feel the need for that conversation to come back to me.

My legs burn as I continue. Although it's not as cold as the night before, the wind whips through my brown work pants as if they were made of silk, the same pants I was wearing when I stormed away from the cottage, and the same ones Henry had cleaned and ready for me when I left his property. My *North Shores* sweatshirt provides only slightly more resistance to the elements, and my shoes are so cold that they feel like they're made of wood. I come to a corner, look at the street sign and see that I'm on Maryland Avenue. I go about a mile further and I can see the dome of the Capital, so I take the next street and veer north. My fingers feel like they're about to crack and the cold has set into my bones. I don't have money to catch a bus and I feel too antisocial to bum, so I find an alleyway and get out of the wind. I stay there for about five minutes, then I get bored and frustrated and I wonder why I'm even trying to stay alive, and I regret the fact that my pistol is back at my house. I walk for another hour.

For some reason that I don't understand, I can't go back home now, despite the fact that that's where I was headed just one day earlier. Even though I live alone, I have an inexplicable feeling that I won't be welcome there. But here, as I walk through a fog of blur and confusion, I feel that I'm worthy of these environs. Perhaps, on a subconscious level, I'm driving myself away from anything that's familiar. Perhaps on a higher level of awareness, I realize what I'm in for and don't want to suffer the humiliation of my errant ways around anyone that knows or cares about me. Perhaps it's a purification, something that I have to go through, something severe enough to make me fly right in the future. I think of Julia and I feel bad that she doesn't know what's happened to me or where I am. Maybe it's better that way though, I think, as I can not guarantee that I'll come out of this. Still, I know that Austin has gotten word to her about whatever happened at the cottage, and after nearly four months she must be sick with worry. I think about my house in Virginia, and how I haven't been there since late May. I know that it's in a good neighborhood, but still I wonder if it's being robbed or vandalized. Still, that's all I do about it—wonder. I am not capable of worry at this point. That's probably a good thing.

The next street is full of shops. I know that I have to get warm, so I begin going into the stores with the intention of browsing until welcome wears thin. I first go into a clothing store and start sifting uselessly through racks of sweaters, trying to escape my boredom by imagining which one I would buy if I had the money. I do this until a young woman comes and, in an arrogant manner, asks if I need anything.

"I'm looking for a Christmas present," I tell her.

"Do you have any money?" she asks condescendingly.

"Yes, I have money," I lie.

She looks at my clothes, and I look down and see that my pants are wrinkled and stained from sleeping outdoors. "Can you show me that you have money," she says.

I'm obviously insulted and in better days I would have blasted her for her rudeness, but I turn and leave without saying a word. I feel defeated, but the warmth of the store has helped thaw my bones and there are other businesses to go into. I enter a shoe store and after the experience I had in the clothing store, I tell the clerk that I don't have much money and that I'm looking for some cheap shoes. He's kinder than the woman and he shows me a selection of what I've asked for and then leaves me alone. Because he was nice to me, I don't want to overextend my welcome and I browse for only a few minutes, then thank him and leave. I cross the street and go into another shop, and when I see it's a jewelry store I know that I won't be able to fake a reason for being in there, so I politely say, "Oops, wrong store," and leave right away.

I manage to kill several hours doing this, but as I have time to think, I contemplate the purpose of such an existence. I ask myself if I'm giving up on life, or if I'm simply biding time while some normalcy returns to me, or if I'm simply too ashamed to go home again. I don't have an answer. Nevertheless, I'm getting hungry and I need to find something to eat. I leave the row of shops behind and continue my walk to the center of D.C.

Feeling self-conscious about my appearance now, I cut through another alley. It's littered with windblown rubbish, but shows few signs of pedestrianism. I go down one block, then cross the street and continue down the alley until I come to a spot where it widens into an opening behind a row of old, four-story brick businesses where six homeless men are huddled around a fire in a trash can. I go up to its warmth without acknowledging them, and I get pushed away by a frail but heavily bearded white man wearing a gray sport coat. Another man grabs my arm and pulls me back toward the barrel. The bearded man storms off, glaring and muttering something at me as he leaves. "Fuck him," the other man says. "I'm Don."

I go to shake his hand, but mine is so frozen that I can't extend my fingers. I tell him that my name is Carl and ask if there's a soup kitchen around, to which he tells me that there is, but that it's closed between one and four. I tell him that I have no concept of time, and he says that it's quarter of three. He introduces me to the other men as I outstretch my fingers near the flames. They are all black, as is Don, and they seem surprisingly normal, with the exception of the man in the sport coat, whom Don says is Banana Dave. He tells me that the crazy lunatic has a thing for flashing, and hence the nickname. The others in the group seem to accept me, and despite the state I'm in, I defy my people phobia and feel oddly at ease with them.

"You don't have a sleeping bag?" a man named Charlie asks. I think it strange that this would be his first question, rather than *What happened to you?* or *What brought you here?* I tell him that I don't have one, and almost ask him how long he's been living like this, but I think how he didn't ask me, so I wonder if it's taboo to talk about such things. He tells me that the soup kitchen has some surplus Army blankets and pillows, and that I can get a warmer coat at the Salvation Army post.

I look around, still exploring my new surroundings, when I notice Banana Dave has come back and is staring at me. He has a psychotic look and I worry about what he might do. I make a mental note not to turn my back to him or fall asleep in his vicinity. As I think this, I'm aware that this is a survival instinct, and with that I realize that I have not given up on myself. I think about the girl at the cottage—the girl whose name has slipped me and, until I can remember her name, I have chosen to call Amy. Perhaps she's the one who's kept me alive all this time. At any rate, the thought of her and the warmth of the fire makes me pledge that I'll fight through whatever is thrown at me.

Four o'clock arrives and Don leads me to the soup kitchen. I trust him more than the others and I want to know how he got here, but I tell myself it's not the time. I already see how the streets can change a person, and although I see no indication that he would do it, I don't want him to flip out because I've asked the wrong question. I follow him through a series of alleys which total about five city blocks and we end up in front of another old, brick building that has Brooks Hardware etched into a square of cement above the door. We go inside and I let out a shiver as the warm air meets my skin. The floor is filled with cafeteria tables that remind me of my elementary school lunchroom, and to the back is a counter where they have soup, rolls and milk ready and waiting. We each pick up a bowl of soup, Don tells me that we are allotted two rolls, I grab two along with a glass of milk, and we head to a table where four others are sitting. A round black woman tells Don that there'll be pizza on Wednesday, donated by some of the Washington Redskins. A man sitting across from me motions with his fingers and nervously mutters, "Name, name, name... c'mon man, what's your name?" His eyes are bulged and intently fixed upon me. I feel uneasy again and have no yearning to start a conversation with another psychopath, but tell him my name is Carl, then put my head down and begin to eat. My surroundings crush me with depression and I want to get the hell out, but I realize that enough time will be spent in the bitter cold, and I know that I don't have many options on the table. I try to distract myself from any negative thoughts, but I wonder how long it will take until the streets make me as fucked up as he is.

We finish eating and I ask Don, "Aren't there any shelters we could stay in?"

"These are hard times, Carl," he tells me with a scowl. "The shelters are all full. You go up and ask the lady for a blanket and a pillow."

"Why can't people stay in here overnight?" I ask.

"Shelters need to meet certain requirements by the district. Because they serve us food here it can't be an overnight facility."

"How about showers?"

"You don't want to take a shower, man. You need all your body oils when you live outdoors. Remember, you're not a big executive or whatever you used to be. Like it or not, you're a man of the streets now, and if you want to survive you have to be street smart."

We head back into the bone-chilling cold. Strangely, I find myself appreciating what I have: my blanket, pillow and the meal I just had. I look at Don, who seems to be in such control of his situation, and I can't hold my question any longer. "What brought you here?" I ask sheepishly.

He reaches into his coat pocket and pulls out a cigarette. "You smoke, Carl?" he asks.

"Not until a few weeks ago," I say, although I don't remember if I do or don't.

"A cigarette after a meal is a good thing," he tells me. "Ain't no need for me to worry about cancer." Then he chuckles and says, "Cancer is my retirement plan." He pulls another out and hands it to me. "I don't give these out to anybody, you know, so enjoy it." He hands me a book of matches and I go next to a building and shield myself from the wind as I light up. I take a deep hit, but the combination of smoke and cold air make me cough to the point of doubling over. I catch my breath and take another drag without inhaling so deeply and I find myself enjoying it, which is something I hadn't done much in the last year or so—enjoy anything. I look over at Don and he gives me a smile, but I don't know if he's smiling because of the cigarette or because he's successfully avoided my question.

As we approach what I decide to call our site, we again come upon Banana Dave. He has a plastic bag in one hand and is digging through garbage cans. He steps in my path as he sees me coming but Don pushes him aside. It's obvious that he's intent on fucking with me and I feel his glare as we press on but I don't look back. Another block and the warmth of the meal leaves my system and again it's bitterly cold. Twilight has set in, and ahead I see the orange flames extending from the burn barrel.

As I warm my body by the fire I think about Amy—and I realize now that that wasn't her name—and how we toasted s'mores at the ocean. I think about those days of youth, and as I do I wish that I could be loving her for what we have, not what we could have had. I wonder how I can remember the distant past so vividly, yet have so much trouble with the past year or so. In a way, I'm glad that I'm somewhat disoriented; I'm sure it makes it easier to cope with this situation. But I sense that time will drag here and I wonder what will happen to me, how long I'll be on the streets and how I'll ever get off of them. I need Don to answer my question; he seems composed out here and I need to know why and how. I think that maybe a few days of this will drive me into an even more muddled state of mind. Still, I have a life force that I know have been bitterly rekindled by Austin's words, even if I can't remember what they were. I feel that there's a reason for me to live, but I don't know what that reason is yet.

As if summoned by the onset of nightfall, everyone in our clan returns to the site and gathers around the burn barrel. We all have plain names—with the obvious exception of Banana

Dave. Besides Don and myself, there's Joe, Barry, Charlie and Gene. Barry appears to be the oldest and I peg him for about fifty-five. Charlie and Gene seem to be around forty, and I figure Don is close to my age. Joe is the youngest, somewhere in his middle thirties, and he has a slight speech impediment. Judging from his weathered look I would guess that Banana Dave has been on the streets for a long time, but it's hard to pin an age on him. I would also guess that he's the only one of us who is totally and irrevocably whacked.

I don't want to be a burden to Don, so I go up to the others and see what kind of conversation I can engage in. "Cold today," seems to be an appropriate opening line, and they all shake their heads and repeat it in a short sentence of their own. I sense no hostility from them so I keep it going and ask when it was supposed to warm up. We engaged ourselves in small talk for a few minutes, then we all stare vacantly into the fire. Eventually Gene says, "We all have to take turns keeping this thing going. Today it was Banana's turn to scrounge. Tomorrow it'll be yours." I nod. "There's a stack of fuel over there," he says, pointing to a three-step stairway to a boarded up entrance. "During the night we have to take shifts. This fire goes out and we'll be freezing."

Night comes and everyone takes their sleeping positions. I fold my blanket in half and sandwiched myself inside. The cement is lukewarm within four feet of the barrel, but outside of that radius it's as cold as Arctic tundra. As I'm nestling in—if you can call a preparation to sleep on the street *nestling*—I'm told that I'll be awakened in three hours to watch the fire. I close my eyes and listen to the wood from an old chair crackle as it burns. I'm worn out and I fall asleep quickly. As I sleep I begin to dream—nonsensical stuff at first—but then I have the most fantastically vivid dream. In this dream I'm at the cottage and taking a stroll along the shoreline. From a mist the girl comes to me, only she's no longer a girl, but a woman. I recognize her immediately and she wears the most caring, loving look that I've ever seen. For some reason I can't bring myself to touch her, even though I long to, but I say her name... Renee... and she smiles as I speak it. Behind her are two shadows, but that's all they are. I try to make them out but she says to me, "It's not time yet, Carl." And that's all she says.

I'm awakened by a kick in the stomach. Feeling disoriented, I look up and see Banana Dave hovering over me, wearing a perverted sneer. "Watch the fire, pisshead," he says in a disgustingly graveled voice. I hold the blanket to my shoulders and stand. It's colder then when I went to sleep, but there is no wind. I exhale and see a solid cloud of breath that doesn't dissolve into the air but stays suspended in front of me. I look inside the barrel and the fire is almost out. The bastard had nearly let the fire die. I feel like kicking him back—partly for revenge, but mostly for the abrupt awakening from my dream—but instead I go up the three steps to where the wood and cardboard are stashed, gather a handful, and quickly return to the barrel while there are still glowing cinders. I tear some of the cardboard into fine pieces and set them in the barrel, then, after they ignite, I place some old chair legs atop of them. The fire takes off and I warm my hands. I'm bored and I don't look forward to doing this; furthermore, I don't know how long my shift is supposed to be, nor do I know whom to awaken for the next shift. I decide to walk down the alley, but as I get to the street I see five guys standing on the corner. I don't know what to make of them and decide to head for the safety of our clan. I hear an ambulance screaming, then listen as it Dopplers itself away. I bring my hands back to the barrel.

I feel fortunate that I'm rather numb to life and I realize that everyone out here needs to be a little insane to survive—even Don. I recall the dream about Renee and nod quickly as I remember now that Renee was her name, and I wonder how I could have ever forgotten. I search for a meaning to it. I wonder why was she an adult in the dream and how I could so realistically visualize her being an adult. I feel awed by the calmness I felt when as she came from the mist. And the two figures. I knew if I thought hard enough I could come up with a supposition for the other factions of the dream, such as the mist and the shoreline, but the two vague figures at each side of her trouble me. Furthermore, it didn't seem to be one of those random, pointless dreams, but rather, a dream with a purpose. What that purpose might be, though, has me befuddled and I wonder why I'd think of Renee, even subconsciously, after so many years. I sigh and throw another board into the barrel.

A week goes by and I'm getting familiar with the streets. In some ways it seems like I've been on them for years. I think about how the cold isn't quite as bothersome and marvel at how quickly I've become acclimated to it. I remember wondering, when I was sane—and in thinking this I admit to myself that I'm not—how anyone could live outdoors in the bitterness of winter. Yet, here I am doing it, and it even seems that time is passing quickly. Christmas is over and I don't have to look at all those happy smiling faces, many of them offering unwanted warm wishes for the holiday season. As much as I hate social interaction, I found this to be downright cruel. What were these people thinking? That they would say, "Merry Christmas to you, sir," and suddenly my world would turn and things would be all right? At any rate, I have a couple days of "Happy New Year," to deal with, and then I can go back to being ignored, ridiculed and loathed.

My thoughts go back a few years and I reflect upon how I used to be. I was highly social and annoyingly responsible. I had my nighttime friends, with whom I knew all the subtleties of cool. I played tennis and racquetball with daytime friends. I was an educator. I had nice things and paid my bills on time. I was a textbook example of a successful suburbanite.

I wonder how I have come to be so comfortable with ignored, ridiculed and loathed.

CHAPTER SIX

A month has passed since I've been on the streets and I feel a dichotomy brewing within me. I've come to find comfort in my situation—certainly not creature comforts, but the certainty and unwavering aspect that my new standing offers me. But I've begun to feel a guilt for becoming complacent with a condition that most everyone finds loathsome. I feel that I have to save myself and I need to do it soon. How I'll do that, though, I haven't a clue. It's early morning, and with the exception of Don who is tending the fire, the others are sleeping. There is the slightest hint of spring in the air—that first day of warmth and melting where the sun shines directly upon the snow—but spring's official first day is still a couple of months away. Yet, I think of the metaphorical phrase *The light at the end of the tunnel,* and I understand it more clearly than I ever have before. Perhaps it's all the contemplating I've been doing; the feeling that, despite my misfortunes, I don't have the incapacity to justify being a street person, and therein lies the guilt.

Don is sitting atop a dilapidated chest-of-drawers which was discarded from one of the shops and into the alley. He holds a styrofoam cup of coffee which he'd panned for earlier, and is looking out toward the awakening city streets. I get up, roll my blanket, and walk up to him. "Mornin'," I say, and he returns my greeting with a nod. He places his coffee on the dresser, jumps down, then takes it and cradles it back in his hands. "You and me are always the early ones, aren't we?" he says.

I don't answer, but say, "I'm feeling something inside... feeling like it's time to move on, but I don't know how anymore."

"I've been feeling that way myself for some time now, Carl. Been thinking 'bout heading down to Florida where the winter isn't so brutal. I'm gettin' too old to be out on these streets year round. Got an aquaintence in Mount Dora, Theo Bell, who once said he'd get me work in the orange groves. They hire migrants and pay 'em cash, so nobody would have to know who I am or where I came from. I could become a new man. But it's been four years since I've seen Theo and I don't even know if he's there anymore. At any rate, I've been playing with the notion of going down there anyway. When I do, you're welcome to join me if you feel so inclined."

I tilt my head in the manner of one who is contemplating, then say, "Let me think about it."

He says, "You think about it, but you think about it quick. I've got a bug in my ass and I ain't waiting for anybody or anything when the right time comes."

"When is the right time?"

"Ideally, it should be a little warmer, I'll be spending some time on the side of the road, and there ain't no shelter from the wind like there is in the city. Have to pan me some money, enough to take a bus out of town—just far enough where folks'll trust givin' a black man a ride."

I looked at the longing in his eyes. I saw how much he, like myself, was ready to take a step up in the world. "If I go, you have to answer one question for me."

"Yes... what brought me to the streets?"

"Yes."

He grabs me by the arm. "Come to the kitchen with me," he says.

We walk silently through the alley, and when we get to the empty parking lot between the alley and the soup kitchen he says, "Was passing through Portland, Oregon and was out on the town. I'd done quite well at the pool table, had pocketed about three-hundred dollars, and I was working my way toward a weekly that I'd rented. It was about one-thirty in the mornin' and there were only a few people out on the streets. I had gone about two blocks when I felt a sting in my back. I dropped to my knees, but knew right away that I was in a fight for my life. I jumped up, faked left and punched the man in the throat with my right. As he gasped for air, he dropped his knife, and I grabbed it and stuck him in the chest. It killed him."

Don stops in the middle of the lot, shamefully looks down at his shoes, then continues. "I ran down to the bus depot with the money I had in my pocket. I was only in the middle of my weekly, but I felt I had to get out of town. I didn't stop to get my belongings—which, looking back, could've been my biggest mistake. For all I know, there was nothin' to connect me with the death of that man 'cept for the fact that I bailed on my stuff and left town. I still don't know if I'm a suspect or if that man was just written off as another thug who had no benefit to society and whose life wasn't worth the trouble of finding out who had taken it. Either way, I haven't given my real name to anybody since then."

I half smile. "So your name's not Don."

"To you and everyone else it is. Because I trust you I've told you way too much already."

We get a plate of biscuits and gravy at the kitchen. They have soda this morning, which is a rarity, and Don grabs one, while I stick with my usual milk. At the table there is a newcomer, a man in his late thirties wearing a gray suit that's been soiled from the streets. He looks at no one as he eats. Again, I find myself curious on how such individuals find their way to where we are. I look at these people to find answers about myself; an attempt to legitimize being here. The man sees me looking and screams, "What the fuck are you looking at?" He pounds his fist on the table and glares through me. I freeze and say nothing, but Don says, "Calm down, mister. You're no different than the rest of us here. I don't care what you used to be, you're a street person now."

Exactly what he had said to me.

The man looks at Don, then back at me. He seems like he wants to reply, but perhaps because of the incorrectness that society has assigned for a white man to argue with a black man, he again lowers his head and finishes his meal without a word.

We head back to our site and I think about going to Florida with Don, what it would be like and if I'd be bettering myself by getting farther away from Virginia. I think about my early-morning realization that I've gotten so deep into this hole that I'm in danger of never coming out, and I now know that the time has come to do something different. But, as with everything else lately, I think too much about it and soon my head begins to spin, so I block the thought out and occupy the rest of the day with the same diversions I've used since I arrived here.

The next day comes and brings with it one of those oddities of nature. To the best of my knowledge, it's the last week of January, but the word on the street this morning is that the temperature sign at First Virginia Federal reads 77°, and that it's the second warmest January day in D.C. history. With the coat I'd gotten from the Salvation Army slung over my shoulder, I take what has become my usual morning walk to the soup kitchen for breakfast. Along the way I see water from melted snow running down the alley, forming a small river that carries the dirt and debris from the winter toward the storm sewer. The 77° oasis prompts me to think more about Don's desire to go to Florida when the weather got a little warmer, and contemplate if God has brought this day for that purpose. I become anxious to run into him; anxious because I've decided that I want to go, too, and I'm hoping he didn't make an early morning exodus.

I find him on the way back. He's just now heading to the kitchen, so I turn and go back with him. He begins talking about how there's a new woman at the site, a pigeon feeder, and he's going on about how he doesn't want a bunch of winged rats hanging around and shitting all over everything. I stop walking and Don looks back at me. "Can we leave today?" I ask.

He seems momentarily perplexed, but then his expression shows that he knows what I'm asking. He doesn't say yes, he doesn't nod, he just pauses for a moment, then says, "We'll leave after lunch."

I spend the rest of the morning walking the streets alone. I feel a desire to take one final look at my last-month's surroundings. I look at the grid on the corner of Maryland and Seventh, the one that would have steam rising from it on a colder day, and grow anxious for the consistency of warmth that Florida will bring. I know it'll be easier to find the pieces of my former life in the sunshine. I continue down into the National Mall, past the Air and Space Museum, all the way to Madison Drive. I stop at a park bench and sit. To my right I can see the white dome of the Capital, and to my left is the Washington Monument. Amidst such edifices of greatness I sit humbly, pondering my foreboding future. I feel out of place, but I force myself to stay. I can't remember when I last respected myself, but I know that I have to start thinking positively. I have to consider myself worthy of being in such a prestigious location. I sit and think until I hear the bells from the National Cathedral ring eleven times.

I begin to walk back. The sun is still bright and I continue to think of spring and better days, and I try to anticipate what the fields of Florida will bring me. I think of the folks that I've panned from and their condescending looks, regardless of whether they gave to me or passed by leaving only scorn. And now I see that look in the faces of everyone I pass on the way back to the site. Florida will be a step in the proper direction— a step toward respectability; yet, I have to realize why I lost that respectability in the first place. Many of the people that frown on me are young enough to have been students of mine— students who in another time would have looked up to me. I had come to avoid eye contact with the people I'd pass, but today I can't help making this observation and I read the faces of everyone that I see along the way: the woman with the proper hair, black fur and trendy glasses, the middle-aged business-man with graying temples that fit his image so perfectly, the younger late-twenties up-and-comers, the professionals finish-ing their careers, already having made their marks—they all look down upon me.

I'm close to the site again and I turn to cross the street. To my left I see a hearse with a funeral procession following it. Inexplicably, I break into a cold sweat. I begin to feel strange— anxious at first, but then panicky. My heart races and every-thing begins to spin, just as in those surreal movie scenes. I don't know what's happening to me and I turn and run—just as I ran when I left the cottage for the streets. I run a block and a half until I come to the alley that links Maryland Avenue to our site, hit the alley full speed and run toward the familiarity of the guys and the burn barrel and the cold cement that sur-rounds it. I'm halfway through the alley when I see the crazy fucker standing in the middle with his arms spread apart in an attempt to block me. He wears the maniacal grin that I see whenever he has me alone. I reach him in seconds and thrust him out of the way with a hard two-handed shove, but I lose my balance from the inertia of the push and I fall to the asphalt. Dave gets up and jumps on me, but I'm full of adrenaline and I easily roll the skinny bastard off of me. I get on top of him and grab his throat. My hands have never felt so strong and hardly a sound escapes as I'm unrelenting in my grip. The veins in his forehead pop out and his face turns a deep red. Just as he begins to lose his will and his body begins to twitch, my shoulder is grabbed and I'm yanked off of him. Without looking to see who did it, I look back at the crazy fucker. He's rolling and kicking, frantically trying to get air, but his windpipe is blocked. I stare at him, not caring if he lives or dies, and then I hear a small squeak of air get through. He looks at me with round, panicked eyes, then doubles over and draws another breath, this one somewhat bigger but still sounding like the phlegm-filled throat of a dying man. Finally, he gasps and gasps again. He collapses to the alley, drained but breathing.

"Hey you," I hear as I feel a light slap on the side of the head. "Are you listening to me?"

I turn and see Don's bewildered stare.

"What the fuck were you thinking?"

I don't know what to say at first, but the rush of the encounter has spared me from whatever I'd been running from—momentarily at least. I realize that I have plenty of latitude with any situation involving Dave, so I shake my head in disgust and say, "I just got fed up with the guy, Don. He said he was going to kill me and I flipped out on him."

The crazy bastard has gotten up and is standing about ten yards away. He heard what I said and seems ready to call me a liar. Still energized, I get up with clenched fists, wide eyes and flared nostrils and take a step toward him, and he turns and runs. He falls as he hits a patch of mud, frantically gets up, rounds the corner and disappears from our sight.

"I can guarantee you that we'll never see him again," Don says. "You put the Fear of God into that boy."

I realize the shortsightedness of Don's comment but don't point it out. He stands with me in the alley until I collect myself. Then, as I come down from my rush, we finalize our plans and we head back to the site.

We get there and see Gene and Charlie talking with the pigeon woman. Gene sees us and approaches, using the 77° as an introductory topic. Don shakes his head in amazement. I'm looking for some reaction from him; some sort of sentiment as he tells this acquaintance farewell, but instead, they continue to talk about the midwinter phenomenon and all the previous weather miracles that have occurred since they've been here. I think about giving him a pat on the back and saying goodbye, but these two aren't letting the temperature thing go and I can't get a word in. Finally, Gene looks over to Charlie and the pigeon woman and asks if they're ready. Charlie nods, and they all take off down the alley. I look back at Gene and Charlie. "You going to tell them?" I ask Don.

"No. None of them need to know."

I feel sort of bad, but I guess that's the way that things work out here on the streets; people come when they're in need and leave when the streets are no longer of use to them. I've come to like Gene and Charlie enough that I'd at least like to wish them well, but I trust Don's street wisdom.

I turn and start for the kitchen, then give Don a head motion to follow. "We better get something to eat. This will be our last sure meal for a thousand miles." He flashes the casual smile of a middle-aged black man. For as much as he conserves emotions, I can tell that he's geared up to take off. We catch our last meal at the kitchen, then Don speaks with Eleanor who is one of the volunteers. She hugs him, so I assume he's told her what we're about to do. From everything I've seen, Don and Eleanor have always been close and I wonder if he's ever slept with her. I wait outside and give him some space, and a bit later he comes out looking sad. "She's the one here that I'll miss," he says. I feel bad for him; he's been here much longer than I have. I know him well enough now that I know he won't want to talk about anything too personal, so I join the 77° chat club as we make our way back through the alley.

The looming trip is providing an adventure that my life has lacked—adventure and a chance to upgrade my standing; something else that's been absent from my recent scheme. We get back to the site and no one's there. I unroll my blanket and roll it tighter, stuffing my pillow inside as I do, while Don takes a last look around. I tie my blanket with a piece of rope that's been at our site, then nod at Don to let him know that I'm ready.

I feel a slight sadness as we leave; this place has been a necessary link between where I was and where I hope to go— the gray space between points A and B. The sentiment doesn't last long, though, and soon we're positioning ourselves on street corners to pan. The spring-like weather seems to have everyone in a good mood and the people are more charitable than usual. I stay on my corner till the five o'clock rush is over, then go back to where Don's standing. We count our money. I suggest we go into a book store and look at a map. We find the travel section, but the clerk is trying to kick us out before we can find what we're looking for, so I occupy the woman while Don slips away. Finally we meet outside, and as we're walking down the street, Don pulls an atlas out of his coat. "I figured they owed us this much for being so rude," he grins.

We browse through the maps and put our route together,

deciding that we'll take a bus from D.C. to Woodbridge, Virginia, then thumb from there. I figure that we've panned for a little more than what we'll need for bus fare and I'm glad that we'll be able to leave today. I stop in a drug store and buy a candy bar, a treat I haven't afforded myself in the time I've been here. We check the schedules at the Greyhound station and find that the bus won't leave till seven-thirty. The out-from-work traffic is still strong, so we head back to our street corners and stay on one corner or another, going back and forth to avoid the cops until six-fifteen. Then I find Don. We've both had a good afternoon.

I suggest we stop at the Y and shower before hitting the road, which Don agrees with, but says that it would be pointless if we didn't get clean clothes, too. We go to the Goodwill on Constitution Avenue and pull clothes from the drop box in back until we each find something that will fit. I'm anxious to throw the clothes I've been wearing away, as they're worn and soiled from the street, and I pray that I'll never again be in such a disgustingly unkempt state.

We make it to the Y just as the sun sets. I throw my street clothes out, with the exception of the winter coat, underwear and socks. I take the latter two into the shower with me and scrub them before washing myself, then dry them under the blow dryer. It feels good to get into clean and different clothes, and again I feel better about myself. I find Don by the front door, talking to an old white man. He spots me and breaks off his conversation and we head for the bus depot.

We go to the counter to buy our tickets, and the woman is disgusted with us as we both unload a pocketful of small bills and change. Nonetheless, we get our tickets and make our way onboard. I realize that at this point we're no different from anyone else on the bus and for the first time in more than a month I am not an obvious street person. I'm hungry, but sleepiness prevails and I nod off before the bus leaves the terminal. By the time I wake we're coming into Woodbridge. I look at Don and he's staring out the window with a peaceful gaze. Again, I don't feel like a vagrant, but like a viable human. I feel the vocabulary that I haven't used coming back to me, and although I can't bring myself to do it, I long to talk to the people around me.

We go into the depot and look at our map, then work our way to the outskirts of town where Highway 1 heads south. The sky is clear and with nightfall it is cold again. My new pants are not as warm as my old ones, the brown work pants I'd bought in North Shores, and I shiver as we wait for a ride. It doesn't come for an hour and forty-five minutes, until a couple of college students pick us up, saying they'll take us just north of Richmond. The two boys appear to be around twenty and both have long hair. The one who's driving has his in a pony tail, but the other one has his down and it looks wild and unkempt, and he reminds me of a street person. But both kids mild-mannered, polite and respectful, and genuinely curious. Don is feeling more loquacious than me and he engages them, and I go back to the comfort I find in silence. So as Don talks with the two kids, I sit, listen, and look out the window and eye the road signs, keeping a bead on how far along we're getting. As I see the exit for Fredericksburg, the town where I was raised, I feel ashamed. *If they could see me now,* I think. The fact is that most of them probably know how screwed up I am anyway. The kids pepper Don with questions, nothing of a personal nature, just small talk. I believe they sense that I don't want to join in and they leave me alone. The chitchat goes on until all involved run out of things to talk about. This is followed by a period of silence which I find most relaxing, and I close my eyes and listen to the R&B station that they've tuned in. The rest of the ride is uneventful and by the time they drop us off it's almost midnight.

We stand at the side of the road with our thumbs out, but traffic is thin, and the cars that do pass us seem to show no interest in picking up two middle-aged adults at such an hour. We're both hungry and tired and we decide to rest in the woods until morning. Don leads the way as we go in twenty yards or so and find a flat, dry patch and settle in there. The ground is soft compared to the cement of the city. I unroll my blanket and spread it out along the flattest part of the forest floor and I fall asleep quickly.

As dawn arrives my stomach is gurgling from a lack of food. I wake up Don, we roll our blankets and head back to the road. The air is crisp, but the sky is clear and it looks like today will be much like the day before. Don's hungry, too, and we try to figure whether to hitch a ride or grab some breakfast first. We walk as we thumb and come upon a donut shop. Problem solved. Then, waiting for a ride, we chat between cars. "You going to miss any of the others?" I ask.

"I'll miss Charlie somewhat." He answers with a chuckle and notices my curiosity, and explains, "Before you arrived, Charlie had a propensity for getting himself incarcerated. He would commit some petty little offense—just something bad enough to get him thrown in for the night. I envied him as I sat and shivered on the street, but with my past history, I couldn't take the risk to do the same." Don smiles to himself, then pulls out a cigarette and turns from the wind as he lights up.

"What about Banana Dave?" I jest.

Don laughs loudly. "Now there is one fucked-up individual, and if I never meet anyone like him for the rest of my life, it'll be too soon."

Our luck befits the splendor of the day as a truck driver pulls over and picks us up. His name is Pete, or Pate, with his accent. I tell him that we're going to Florida and he says he'll take us all the way to Savannah, which is more than halfway to Mount Dora. He's a big man with broad shoulders, callused hands and a yellow-toothed smile, and is friendly and genuine. He wears a Carhart jacket with a flannel shirt underneath and seems to enjoy talking about politics in a salt-of-the-earth type manner. As we head down the road we talk more. Don works the fact that we're hungry into the conversation without telling him our exact plight, only saying that we're a little low on cash. Pete says he has to keep on schedule, but when we get to Raleigh he buys us each a meal at a truck stop.

Don looks around as we walk in. It's the first time I've eaten at a restaurant in a long time, but I wonder how long it's been for him. We walk to a table. As we do, no one looks at us any differently than they would anyone else. I feel my ego move up a notch on the normalcy scale. I order the breakfast I always used to have, scrambled eggs and sausage with a side of toast. The sun is shining, the food is familiar, and the bitter streets of Washington D.C. are two-hundred miles behind me.

Pete gets up to use the rest room, and while he's gone, Don and I fill our pockets from a bowl holding an assortment of crackers and breadsticks. It seems strange as I do this, to scrounge food and not be either begging or stealing, but as I think this, I reach over to the table behind us and empty that dish as well. I give half to Don and we go back to our breakfasts while we wait for Pete to return. We finish eating and, despite Pete's hurry, he takes a couple minutes and sips coffee while waiting for his meal to settle. As he does this, he asks what prompted us to go to Florida.

"We were laid off from a sheet-metal factory in Rockville," Don answers without hesitating, as though he had anticipated the question and rehearsed for it. "I've been out of work for almost a year now and lost almost everything I owned. Carl here was in the same boat, he was my shift partner at the plant, and we thought that if we were gonna be poor, at least we'd be poor and warm if we tried our luck down south."

Pete adds something about how it's that way all over and makes some comment about the fucking Republicans. We both kind of shake our heads and agree, not out of accordance, but because the man was nice enough to give us a ride. I'm anxious to go, as I'm hoping Pete doesn't ask me anything about sheet metal. He finishes his coffee, we go back to his rig and again we're on the road. As we ride, I again try to anticipate the role Florida will have in my rehabilitation. All I know are two things: that I'm not ready to return home—be that my house in Virginia or the cottage in Delaware, and that I still have many issues to deal with. I made up my mind that when I do return, I want to have things straightened out. I recall that I had happiness and stability in my past, even though I don't remember the particulars of it. I recall having friends, and I remember being respected. I feel that things are on the rise, and I vow that I will never again allow myself to sink to such a desperate level. In my mind, I count the things I have to gain back: my self-respect, economic stability, and my religion, or at least a sense of who God is. How could he, after all, have let me go through what I did, or for that matter, any of the others I'd met on the street. But the thing I feel most in need of is to gain total memory of my past. I sense something tragic may have happened to me and I have to deal with that before anything will appear entirely normal again. For now, however, I put the issues to rest, close my eyes and listen to Johnny Cash on AM radio and the rhythm of the road.

CHAPTER SEVEN

The night passes quickly as I drift in and out of sleep. Pete's in a hurry to get to Savannah and he's pushing the pedal. Don climbed in back at the last stop; his snoring clashes with the country music on the radio as we roll down I-95. I sit and stare at the stream of lights heading north, listening to an occasional story about the road and taking a break from thinking about the future. Pete had fueled up just south of Fayetteville. There, we stretched our legs a little and went into the truck stop for a late night coffee, but we've been rolling steady ever since. The night air is crisp but pleasant. I have my window cracked and the smells of the South permeate the cab and clash with Pete's body odor. We crossed into South Carolina about an hour ago, and Pete tells me that we have about a hundred and ten miles until he has to drop us off, north of the city, as I requested.

I'm getting used to the road now and it's good to be out of Washington. I again notice how I feel more respectable; after all, if I look a little grubby, people would perceive it as the look of a road-weary man. I reach to the floor and grab our atlas, snatch a cigarette lighter that's laying on the dash, then find the

Georgia map. Through the flickering flame, it looks to be about one hundred-twenty miles from Savannah to the Florida border. I turn back a page to the Florida map and guess it to be one-fifty from the border to Mount Dora. I add the distances and get two-seventy, which could take us anywhere from four hours to two weeks to navigate, depending on how lucky we are at thumbing.

I come back from my thoughts to hear Pete in the middle of a story, something about a bar brawl in a Cleveland pool room. "The guy who had the table had been in the Marines. Everything was Marine this and Marine that. The guy with his money on the table told him to shut the fuck up and play and GI Joe took exception to it. He takes his cue with both hands, the way one would hold a barbell, and shoves it under his throat, saying, 'Tell me to shut up now.' Well, to GI Joe's misfortune, the other guy had been taking steroids for the past ten years and it'd screwed with his head, and he knees old Joe in the balls, takes the cue stick and pushes him backwards over the pool table, chomps onto his nose and rips most of it off with his teeth. Then he turns to the crowd and spits the guy's nose onto the floor, and with bloody teeth yells out, 'Come on! Who's next?' I don't know what happened after that; I figured it was a good time for me to leave." Pete chuckles a little, then grabs his styrofoam coffee cup and has a gulp. I recall the story that Don had told me and make a mental note to stay out of pool halls.

The temperature drops as the night passes and the cold flow of air from the opened window is stiffening my neck, but Pete's unpleasant smells force me to keep it open. Along with the body odor problem, he's developed gas from his meal at the truck stop. He laughs and makes sophomoric comments whenever he releases it, as I'm left to deal with the aftereffects.

It's another half-hour before Don wakes. He pokes his head

into the front seat and asks where we are. Pete tells him that we're an hour out of Fayetteville, looks at Don for a reaction, laughs, then tells him that we're really about fifty miles from Savannah. Don sits up and through a deep stretch and yawn asks me if I got any sleep. I tell him that I didn't and that I feel wide awake, which I do, thanks to the constant stream of cold air rushing past my face.

We roll uneventfully for the next forty-five minutes. As we approach Savannah, the traffic picks up, even though it's near three in the morning. We cross the Georgia state line. Two miles later Pete takes an exit ramp and pulls to the side of the road. "Here you go, north of the city just as you requested, signed, sealed and delivered," he says. I shake his hand as I thank him and stand alongside the rig as I wait for Don, who likewise thanks Pete for the ride. As Don shuts the door, I see Pete's face drop. I feel bad—for as likable as he is, I get the impression he's a lonely fellow. As he pulls away I wonder if he has anyone in his life: a wife or significant other, kids, close friends. I think about how being on the road must make for a lonesome life. Quite a thought, I think, for someone who has spent much of the last year and a half running away from any kind of social interaction.

And again here we are—Don and I at the side of the road, searching for our ride to a different life. He's still a bit groggy from the nap and I'm beginning to wish I had taken one. But the night air will undoubtedly keep me awake, even though it's not quite as cool without it rushing in through the truck window. I turn to Don and ask him how he's doing and he mumbles something inaudible. I think nothing of it and assume he's still in the process of waking up. We slowly walk down the road for a few minutes before I say, "The traffic really thinned out with this exit, hey?"

He stops in his tracks. "Of course it thinned out you idiot!"

His response surprises me; I've never had him raise his voice to me before. "What gives?" I ask.

"I'll tell you what gives. What the hell were you thinking, telling that truck driver to drop us off north of the city? Anyone passing by here will be going into Savannah. We don't want to go into Savannah. We want to go south! If we get dropped off south of the city then we have cars passing by that are going in the direction we want to go. But no! Here we are heading right into fucking Savannah, Georgia."

I get the point after the second sentence, but wait out his tirade before acknowledging my mistake. "I'm not used to hitch-hiking... sorry. I'm used to driving myself, and when I did I always stopped for the night just short of the city—north of it if I was traveling south and south of it if I was traveling north."

"Well, you ain't doing the driving this time, are you?"

I shake my head in disgust at his persistence. "I said I was sorry, man. It's not that big a deal, is it?"

He doesn't answer and we walk for a half hour without anyone saying anything. The thin traffic concerns me and I feel that getting us south of Savannah is now my responsibility. I regret not having used my head, and even more, regret the timing of making a misjudgment. I was just beginning to trust myself again, just beginning to feel a little normal, and now I'm left questioning this, which avalanches into questioning everything. I torture myself with this self-imposed inquisition until I realize my purpose on this voyage—to move forward and assimilate. I force myself to focus on the present. *We're out of D.C. and we're already in a warmer climate. I'll be getting a job and earning money again, and from there I'll think about where my life can go and how I can get there. So we're north of the city. Big fucking deal; I've been sleeping on the fucking streets!*

We come up to a convenience store with a bench out front.

Without saying anything, we both head toward it as if by instinct. We sit down and Don pulls out a cigarette, lights it and hands it to me. "Sorry if I was a little hard on you back there," he says.

I nod and tell him it's okay.

He lights a smoke of his own, then, looking straight ahead into the black nothingness, says, "The day we met, you asked what brought me to the streets. It took a long time, but I finally told you. Now, it's my turn to ask you. What brought you to the streets, Carl?"

I hadn't expected this question from him. I've been trying to answer it myself and haven't come up with any kind of logical reason. I turn and shrug my shoulders. "I really don't know," I say with the wide-eyed honesty of a six year-old. "If you only knew how much time I've spent thinking about that question. I used to be successful. I was a college professor, I had lot of friends, a nice house and an expensive car. Something happened that brought me from that point to where I am now, but I don't know what that something is."

"Was it Renee?" he asks in a gentle, slow, black man's voice.

My eyes widen. "How do you know about her?"

"I don't know about her, but you say her name frequently when you sleep."

I suddenly feel closer to him—that feeling one gets with a stranger when they share a common acquaintance. The simple fact that he said her name made it seem like he actually knows her. Again, I contemplate how a girl that I knew for a brief period of my life could have such an impact that my thoughts keep going back to her.

"You all right, man?" I hear him ask.

"Yeah... yeah," I say, and I try to come up with some kind of reasonable answer to his question. I begin again. "I don't know what brought me here, but I think Renee may be part of the reason. There's something that I'm blocking out, I'm sure. The distant past I remember well, and I remember everything that happened after I arrived in Washington. It's the year and a half to two years before I got to D.C. that I'm having a problem with."

Don clears his throat in the manner of someone who's about to say something that he doesn't know if he should, then says, "Maybe something terrible happened, and maybe this Renee girl was part of it."

I sigh and drop my shoulders in defeat. "I just don't know what to tell you, Don. I don't even know myself."

He finishes his cigarette and gives it a flick. He doesn't get up as he usually would, rather, seems content to sit for awhile. I'm fine with this, considering the weighty question that has resurfaced. The last thing I feel like doing right now is catching a ride with some jabbering stranger. Besides, morning will provide a better opportunity for finding a southbound ride.

Through the dim light I look towards the woods across the highway from us. The warm temperatures of the day have brought out the smells of the South, as if it were a fragrant candle whose scent was released by the heat of its flame. There is an indigenous smell down here, just as the North Woods can be identified by the scent of damp leaves covering its forest floor, and the Atlantic coast has its distinctive salty, sea-air smell, and the desert Southwest's dry arid air is uniquely its own. When you catch hint of a certain smell it alerts the senses to where you are. Now, I obviously know where I am geographically, but when I get a drift of southern magnolia, the feel of the South settles within me.

Don, who had been sitting quietly for several minutes, turns back to me and prods further about why I went homeless. "You know, I've seen a lot of fucked-up individuals out there—people who walk the street all day talking to themselves, shell-shocked paranoids who jump when you touch them, psychopaths like Banana Dave, those with hollow, empty eyes... I've seen them all, Carl, and you ain't one of them. Sounds to me like something bad happened to you, and once you face it, you'll get back to wherever it was that you were."

I find encouragement in his words. If he sees me as something less than totally whacked, then perhaps I should look at myself in that light as well. I make that my focus; to quit looking at myself as a lost cause and try to isolate the situation that brought me here, deal with it, and then move on. And it seems that this process must begin with Renee. I have to figure out why I've been thinking about her so much lately, and I have to interpret the haunting dream with her and the two shadowy figures. I think back to the past and try to recall my relationship with her in chronological order. I go back to 1971 and seeing her from afar, then meeting her as I walked along the seashore. I recall the next time I saw her, 1974, and the two of us hanging out, making daily trips to the diner in North Shores, kissing her for the first time, and having our nightly bonfire. I remember talking about either joining the Peace Corps or going to college, promising that whichever one we chose we'd do it together. I know I didn't join the Peace Corps—I attended The University of Maryland—but I don't believe she was there with me. And this is what befuddles me. For as close as we were, and as much as she's in my thoughts now, I should remember whether or not we attended the same college. I remember my curriculum and I remember graduating. I remember moving out to Vermont and every teaching job I had thereafter. I remember little things, too, like going to baseball games and concerts, or traveling to distant places, and I remember the minor, insignificant things that make up the bulk of one's existence. I seem to remember everything except the point that Renee exited my life, and with that, I'm convinced that Don is onto something.

I dig deeper into my last thought and dissect it item by item. I start with college, then go onto my work life. From there I think about all my leisure and recreational activities. In each instance I can remember other people that I associated with, but I can't recall Renee being part of any of it. I can't even remember having a phone conversation with her. Another thing that strikes me is that I can't remember being with any women physically since I was in high school, which seems odd because I've always found the female body attractive and I know I'm not a bad looking guy. I continue my analysis like a detective preparing a case for a jury. I go back to my statement to Don that it's the last year and a half to two years that I'm having trouble remembering, which is true. In this period of time, I don't recall much at all. I don't know what I did for a living, who I associated with, or any of the aforementioned insignificant things that I did in my leisure. I get a strong feeling that there's a key hidden within this realization. I try to put the two eras together. In the first era I can remember everything except for Renee, with the exception of our original encounters at the cottage, that is. In the latter era I can't recall much of anything that happened to me before I got to D.C., aside from fixing up the cottage and helping Henry at the farm. I'm beginning to feel overwhelmed and everything begins to spin. I lower my head between my legs and hold it with both hands.

"You okay, man?" Don asks.

I turn to him with a distressed look. "I have to walk," I say, and I rise from the bench and head towards the seclusion of the woods across the highway. I was so close to a revelation before Don spoke, but the interruption sent my thoughts scattering in every direction. I try to reassemble what I had deduced. After a few minutes of walking I have them collected and I summarize; *no memory loss in early adult years except for the existence of Renee, and not much recollection at all from the past two years.* I feel caught up with where I was and proceed from there, trying to find some link or pattern. I feel like I'm authoring a case study for a mental health magazine: *Why I'm So Fucked Up, by Carl H. Morgan.*

I hear rustling ahead of me and see a deer dart from the edge of the road to the safety of the woods. I again force myself to focus. Then I have a dramatic moment—a compilation of all the facts that I know to be true, blended with the conjecture of the unknown that I must rely upon: *Renee must have died!* I stop walking and feel that cold sweat come upon me again—the same sweat I felt when I saw the hearse, and now I remember it to be the same cold sweat I felt when I ran from the cottage. I force myself to stay composed. As fast as my mind is racing, I know that I can't block this realization out and pretend it didn't happen. If this is true, it explains everything—why I can remember the distant past except for her, and why I can't remember anything for the near past. This, too, leads me to conclude that she must have been killed in the beginning of that period of time dating back to the last year and a half to two years. My heart rate must be up to one-fifty; yet, I need to know what her role was in my life. I take a breath and concentrate, and conclude that she must have had a significant one for me to react like this.

I stop and turn around. I feel drained to the point where I could drop to the ground. I can't take any more thinking, and instinct makes me leave my progress at this for the night. And it's enough for now. I drop to my knees, but it was good. For the time being, I'll assume that my assumption is correct. Next time I'll try to figure out what my last contact with her was and what kind of relationship we had. And hopefully I can find something to disprove this theory. I feel sad that the beautiful girl from my youth may be dead, but now my body has the

80

tremor of fatigue, and I feel the responsibility of keeping myself from falling back into the depths of denial. I owe that to myself and I owe it to Don. He doesn't need to be burdened with somebody who's falling apart. I'll take my steps slowly. I'm ready to return to the matters of this night and get back on the road.

I cross the highway when I come to the convenience store. Don sees me and comes my way. He looks worried, but I tell him everything's all right. "I'm sorry I brought that shit up," he says.

"It's okay," I tell him. "I'm glad you did."

CHAPTER EIGHT

The sound of thunder awakens us. I get up and brush the dirt and leaves off my back and take a leak. Going to the edge of the woods, I look up at the ominous sky; it looks like the rain will come soon and that it'll be an all day affair. Don had been sneezing much of the night, and seeing that he's sleeping comfortably now I decide to let him rest, and I walk across the street to the convenience store. I dig the loose change out of my pocket and find a dollar twenty-five—enough for a large cup of coffee, which I'll share with Don. I sit on the bench outside the store and drink my half first; I don't particularly care to catch his cold. Anyway, it'll give him more time to rest.

As I sit and wait for the rain to fall, I briefly think about the revelations of the previous night, but instinct reminds me to let it simmer some before digging into it again. Instead, I try to figure how we're going to get across town. Don was justified, if not right, to yell at me. It was stupid to ask Pete to drop us off here. Furthermore, the clothes we got at Goodwill are now wrinkled and dirty from sleeping outdoors and once again we'll look like bums—making the task of getting a ride all the more difficult.

After a nearby lightning strike I decide it's time to get Don up and out of the woods. It occurs to me that during the time I've know him, this was the first time that he wasn't awake before me. I shake him till he wakens and tell him that a storm's coming and that we should get indoors. He sits up, wipes the drool off his chin with his sleeve, and I hand him the remainder of the coffee. "What's that you say about rain?" he asks, not sounding quite awake.

"A good storm's brewing—thunder, lightning and all that. We better get inside."

He takes a drink, slowly considering what I said. "I think we'd be better off trying to hitch a ride before it rains. Who wants to pick up a wet hitchhiker?" He takes another sip, then looks up at me. "I think we should at least give it a try. Then if we don't have any luck we can still go inside when the rain starts."

I nod. He's right again. I begin to feel like a clumsy encumbrance. Were he traveling alone, he probably would have caught a ride last night; he would've had Pete drop him off on the south end of the city and he'd be halfway to Mount Dora by now. We walk out to the highway and wait thumbs-up by the side of the road as the thunder continues to rumble. It's another twenty minutes before the rain comes. We haven't gotten a ride, so we head for the convenience store and wait under the awning until it lets up. I get a shiver as a cold front has come along with the storm, and suddenly, even though we've migrated south, our oasis of spring is gone and once again it's late January.

The first hour passes swiftly. Don's getting restless and is dropping hints that we should brave the elements and return to the side of the road. I ignore these hints until I sense that he's getting aggravated with me, and I remember that the inspiration for this undertaking was his not mine and I ask him outright if he's ready to start hitching again. Another hour passes and nobody will pick us up. The good thing about being in the rain, though, is that it no longer shows that we had slept outdoors. We are just rain soaked hitchhikers.

Another hour and the rain seems to be letting up some. We're both hungry and we head back to the convenience store, where Don gives the laid-off sheet metal story to the owner, and asks if there are any little jobs we can do in exchange for food while we wait out the rain. He's sympathetic and gives us sandwiches and a side dish from his deli and tells us to eat first and that he'll find a task or two for us afterwards. I'm so nutritionally depleted that I can almost feel my body absorbing the food before it gets to the pit of my stomach. We finish eating and the man has us restock his beer and soda cooler, and then give it a good moping. It only takes forty-five minutes, but he gives us each a ten for good measure. And it's at that point that a feeling of encouragement rushes over me and I sense that we will make it to Florida.

The rain is now only a drizzle, but clouds in the western sky tell us that it will eventually let loose again. We thank the shop owner for his Georgian hospitality and get back to the side of the road. Finally we are picked up. It's an old, rural man with a wet, smelly dog, but I don't care the least. He stutters when he talks and is hard to understand, so neither Don nor I extend the conversation more than what's necessary; we only nod to most everything he says. He mumbles something about fixin' somethin' for his sister in Belfast and that he'll drop us off at the off-ramp. I wholly assume that he's still talking about Georgia and that he hasn't succumbed to senility.

He was. We come to the exit and he delivers us as promised. The mangy dog who had been licking me for the duration of the ride tries to get out, and the old man jerks out a stutter and the dog retreats to the floorboard. We both wave as he drives away, then head across a field from the off-ramp to the on-ramp. As luck would have it, there's a prison crew on cleanup detail, supervised by two rifle-toting guards. Don grabs my arm and pulls me back. "I can't chance this, man," he says. I hadn't seen any signs that prohibit hitchhiking, but with his past and the alias he must use, I understand his uneasiness.

We head back through the field. Don's getting paranoid. "If we could see the guards then they could see us, and they're going to wonder why we doubled back."

"Then we need to go back down there," I say.

Don pauses. "But by now we'll have gone back and forth too many times not to look suspicious." We stood there as he thought, behind the cover of a cresting knoll and temporarily out of sight, and for the first time I saw indecisiveness in my friend. Something from my past resurfaces, an inner clearness that gives me an innate idea of what should be done, and I sense that we needed to go forward. Despite my poor judgment in getting us dropped off at the north end of Savannah, not to mention the overall and ongoing questions I have about myself in general, I coax Don into following me. "They're prison guards, not police," are the words that ultimately convince him. We go down the on-ramp. I notice the prisoners eyeing us as if we're one of them as the draconian guards bark orders for them to get back to their task. We stay quiet as we move toward them, occasionally turning at the sound of a vehicle to thumb. I think how the sight of prisoners has to be a deterrent to anyone who'd ordinarily be prone to giving us a ride, and I sense that we may not get one until we either put distance between us and them or until their work detail is finished.

I can tell Don is thinking his steps—methodically acting out when to look around, how to carry himself, when to turn to me and say something quite insignificant—and he looks stiff and unnatural, or perhaps even guilty. I try to loosen him up by reacting in an effervescent way to whatever he says, even though we both understand that the words are but a bridge to get out of eyesight of the guards. I try to comprehend what he's going through. I think of how horrible it must be to fear lifelong incarceration and to have that fear personified and within twenty yards of you. Finally we come to the first guard; a stern, stout, black man. We both say hello and he acknowledges us with a nod. I relax. We won't have a problem.

Several more hours pass. The rain has resumed and the lunch we had at the convenience store has worn off and a road-weary feeling is hovering over both of us. However, the temperature has risen to what I'd guess to be 55°. I think back to Washington and realize how fortunate I was that all the precipitation we experienced was in the form of snow, and not that cold rain that falls on a 35° day.

It isn't until around eight in the evening that we get a ride. This time it's a man in his early-thirties who appears to be gay. We get in and he asks where we're headed. He sounds gay, too. Don tells him with a laugh, "No farther than Mount Dora, Florida."

"Well I can't do that for you," he says in a whiny voice, "but I can take you as far as Jacksonville."

"Jacksonville would be great," Don says, and I ask, "How far is Jacksonville from where we are now?"

"Well it depends on what you want to call Jacksonville; it is the largest city land-wise in the United States. If you're talking from here to the city limits then it's about a hundred and twenty miles, but add another twenty or so to get to the middle of town."

I thank him and lean back in the back seat. Don and I resume our roles of loquacious guy, quiet guy, although I believe Don, too, senses that this guy's gay, and isn't as forward as he has been with the others who have given us rides. I hear the driver tell Don that he's a salesmen for a pharmaceutical company and that he goes to Jacksonville once a week. Don gives the now-standard laid-off sheet metal worker story, this time elaborating on it further by saying that the plant had been bought out by a Chinese company who brought in their own cost cutting management staff. I fight to keep from chuckling. After two hours we're in the heart of Jacksonville and the man pulls over to the curb and lets us out. "By the way," he say as we're bidding him farewell, "I'm not gay—just so you know. I have a wife and two kids." He reaches over and pulls the door shut before either of us can respond, leaving us standing speechless on the sidewalk.

We take a look at our surroundings. The streets have that old Florida look to them and it feels good to at least be in the state of our destination. Don sees a party store across the street and we head for it. The ten dollars may have to last us until we get to Mount Dora, so I'm thrifty in satisfying my hunger and feed myself on two dollars and forty-nine cents. I crave a soda, but the street person in me comes back out and I opt for going into a bar and asking for a glass of water. Don digs out his map and we go over the route again. We find a city bus and pay pocket change for it to take us to its southernmost stop, where we'll negotiate our way onto U.S. Highway 17.

On the bus, Don and I decide that we'll take some time before going thumbs-up again. We're rested from the last ride, but a little tired of the process. Besides, it's late night now and our chances of landing a ride have diminished. There's a street bench in front of a liquor store and we take it, and the familiar feeling of being a street person again comes over me. But I don't mind, as I feel comfortable doing this perhaps one or two more times with the knowledge of respectability in sight. As we sit I realize that, outside of going into the bar and only ordering water, I hadn't thought of myself as anything less than normal until this point of the day.

Eventually, Don falls asleep on my shoulder, and perhaps because of the perception of the man whom I had thought to be gay, and the way it would look now to any passersby, I nudge him till he wakens. He wipes his mouth and shifts his lean to the other direction. I turn and lean opposite to him and begin watching the life of the streets until I, too, nod off.

I guess it to be around four in the morning when I wake. I feel hungry again and I eye a gas station. It's still open. I turn to Don, but he's sleeping soundly. Furthermore, he has snot that has run past his lips and down to his chin. I'm grossed out at the sight, but remind myself that it's only because he's sick and leave him there while I go for another snack. I wander the streets as I eat, then return to the bench. It's not until around six that Don wakes up. We stay on the bench for a bit, until he notices a cop doing morning patrol. Then he grabs a bite and we head for Highway 17.

After walking the first five miles we get a ride; again with a trucker. He's an ordinary man with a picture of Jesus on his dashboard. Perhaps because of the picture, Don eliminates the sheet metal plant lie from his routine and we ride quietly into DeLand, leaving us a mere thirty miles to Mount Dora.

The feel of the Deep South presides, as we begin walking down state highway 42. The skies are clear and the temperature is near perfect, but it looks like they've gotten a significant amount of rain here over the past several days, more by far than what we'd experienced north of here. It takes us about a half-hour to get out of town and into rural Florida. The traffic is thin, but the walk isn't cumbersome. In fact, I feel content to walk for awhile before getting picked up. We pass a gas station with a marquis sign that says Dr. Pepper 40¢. We stop and I grab one, while Don buys a Coke and a small loaf of home-made bread.

Morning turns to afternoon and we haven't been picked up.

I guess that we've been walking for three plus hours. We've been keeping a good pace and I estimate that we've traveled about fifteen miles on foot since we were dropped off in DeLand. An hour later a flatbed carrying a tractor pulls over. We get on the back and he takes us into Mount Dora.

We get off in the middle of town. Architecturally, it has a Spanish feel to it. The white stone buildings are as square as the city blocks and as clean as the pristine streets. Don walks into a hardware store and asks the location of the plantation, whereupon he is told that there are several of them in the area. He mentions Theo Bell's name, but to no avail. The man he's talking to asks if we're looking for work, then suggests that we try the largest one, as they would be most prone to be hiring. He tells Don to take Main Street all the way through town, then once we pass the city limits sign, take the first dirt road on the right.

We come to the dirt road—the quarter-mile link between the streets of D.C. and our final destination. Despite the torrential rains of the past two days, the road is firm and good to walk on. The air is thick and the smells a confusing combination of soil, magnolia, and watermelon. Don is showing the wear of our journey and wipes his brow often. My muscles are sore, but I feel strong. I guess that we've walked thirty miles or more over these last three days.

As the road makes its last turn, the plantation comes into sight. I ask Don to tell me more about Theo Bell. He tells me that he's a man of integrity, and that if he put a good word in for us we would certainly be hired. That eases my mind somewhat—not that a job in the orange groves was the do-all-end-all for me, but again, that necessary step toward getting home. After hearing about Theo, I'm curious about him, what he looks like, what his demeanor might be, and how he'll receive me.

The road ends with a turnaround in the front of a red barn,

the vastness of which is of plantation-days proportion. We nose around the outside, peering in each door while looking for someone who looks like he could help us. The people we see are all grunts, though, general laborers, most of whom appear to be Mexican. Don has taken more command of the situation, and while he goes inside I look across the endless fields that lay in front of me and to my right. Behind me are orange trees, their vastness of number equally phenomenal to the seemingly perpetual field in front of me. To the left are three rows of migrant housing, each row about a full city block in length, and the way everything is laid out, the plantation has the feel of a self-contained community. I walk around the corner of the barn to get a better look at what I presume will be our accommodations. Small children run back and forth, between and around the houses, as freely as if they were playing in the streets of Juárez, or Nogales, or any of the other border towns that Julia and I had visited on teenage vacations with our parents. A couple of women hang clothes on a line, their Spanish voices rattle fervently as they entertain themselves from the drollness of their task.

I see Don coming out of the barn and I go to find out what's happening. "Theo isn't here anymore," he reports. "But the man in there says that we need to talk to Morris."

"Morris," I repeat. "First name or last?"

"Humph," Don mumbles. "Never clarified that."

We follow a trail that leads to a small metal building that serves as an office. Inside there are two metal desks with folding chairs. The front desk is occupied by a woman in her forties, who I assume is the secretary to the man sitting at the desk that faces the side wall. Don tells her that we're looking for Morris. She turns, and in a thick southern accent, she says, "Mr. Morris."

The man behind the other desk rises, and on his way toward

us he asks, "You two together?"

"Yes," Don says as I nod.

"I pay three bucks an hour and provide housing. No benefits, no insurance. You work twelve hours a day, six days a week. You get Sundays off."

Don shoots me a glance and I approve with another nod. "We'll take it," Don says.

"It's too late today for you to do anything, but you'll begin in the morning." He turns towards his secretary. "Jan, call Richardson." She has the phone in her hand before he finishes and pages Mike Richardson over the loudspeaker.

Morris turns back to us and says, "Richardson will show you your shack and tell you where to meet him in the morning. He'll be your contact person. I don't need you to come to me for anything. If you have a problem, he'll take care of it. If he can't, you can leave at any time. Jan has payroll, which can be picked up after Fridays shift. Any questions?"

I speak up. "How did you know that we were looking for a job?"

He flashes a slight smile that forms on one side, as Don stares at me with eyes that tell me to keep my mouth shut. "You don't look like bankers to me," he finally says, and he turns, goes to his desk and takes a drink of his coffee.

We silently stare out the window as we wait for Richardson to arrive. When he shows up, he only asks for our last names. He's a tall, thin, fair-haired man in his early thirties, but he has a hardened face and a stern demeanor. He wears fades jeans that are caked with dried mud from the knee down, work boots that are just as muddy, and a tank top. As I look closer, I see that he has some sort of growth on the left underside of his cheek, and I catch myself staring so I look at my feet, and when I do, I realize that the penny loafers I'd gotten from the Salvation Army will be less than ideal for this situation. Still, compared to laying on a frozen street in January, I don't think mud will bother me.

Richardson leads us down a path cut through the weeds that takes us to our quarters, a small shack with the number 18 stenciled on the door. Inside, it looks even smaller; I guess it to be about twelve-by-twenty. There are two beds, two dressers, a toilet and a tub. On the left there's a small kitchen area with one hanging cabinet, a sink, a small oven and refrigerator. The walls and ceiling are plain and the paint on them is chipping onto the well-worn blue and white linoleum flooring. There is one window in front to the left of the door and another in the bathroom; the buzz of flies is heard from both of them. Richardson hands Don the key and we follow him outside. "When you boys leave, you'll get your last pay after we inspect your quarters. If it's not torn up and filthy, then you'll get paid. There's a van that goes into Mount Dora three times an evening: at five-thirty, seven and eight-thirty. There's one Sunday van that goes in at nine in the morning and comes back at noon, for those of you who like to go to church," he adds with a sneer. "If you take any of these, you have to come back on the van you came on, or take a cab or walk. In town, there's a grocery store, laundry and a couple bars. You can drink all you want, but if you cause any trouble here, you're out. Any questions?"

I halfheartedly raise my hand like a shy grade school kid, and tell him that we are flat broke and I ask if we can get a small advance for food. Richardson shows a rough exterior, but I see he has a heart when he pulls out a twenty, telling me to make sure he gets it back first thing Friday evening.

As he heads back toward the fields, I guess it to be around three o'clock. I try to recall the times the van goes into Mount Dora, but I'm not sure and I ask Don.

"Five-thirty, I believe," he says. And we should probably catch that one and get some food. We've got ten each, and it has to last two and a half days."

I turn, go back inside and flop on the bed that lies to the right. It feels good to lay on a real bed and I close my eyes. Through the sweet smell of watermelon and the buzz of flies and Mexican children, I fall asleep. It isn't long before Renee comes to me again. This time we're back in an apartment in Burlington, sitting on the porch as a cool breeze comes off Lake Champlain and blows her shoulder-length brunette hair against my face. I pull it back and go to kiss her, but she stops me, gets up and motions for me to follow her. We go inside and into a small room with a crib. She picks up a crying toddler, and as she faces me again, I notice that she's pregnant. She rubs her belly and smiles at me, then she waves, and the toddler waves, and just as before, they vanish into a mist. I go out to the porch and there's an envelope where we were sitting. I pick it up and pull out a card that says, *HAPPY BIRTHDAY, DANIEL*. On the front is a picture of a little boy riding a bike through the woods. The boy is older, about ten, and he looks familiar. The sun is bright and there are birds and flowers all along the trail he's riding on. I open the card and on the inside there's a car that's been in a horrific accident. The front end is smashed all the way to the front seat, the doors are crumpled and all the glass is broken. I recognize the vehicle immediately and I begin to tremble.

I'm awakened by Don shaking the bed. "Man, you must have had quite a dream there, soldier, but we got to get going if we're going to catch that ride."

I'm sweating profusely and feel shaken and disoriented, and it takes me a moment to even realize where I'm at. I get up and go into the bathroom—just to be alone. I look at my distressed face in an old mirror that hangs opposite the door. "Daniel," I murmur. "And Prudence." I drop to my knees and break down."

Don hears me and knocks on the door, then comes in when I don't answer. "What's wrong, man?" he asks. I hear him but can't answer or look at him. He puts his hand under my armpit and coaxes me up. "I don't know what's with you, man, but you have to pull it together. This is our first day here and the other people are gonna think we're some kind of freaks."

I sob, then take some toilet paper and blow my nose. I know I've had another revelation—an important and much-needed breakthrough—and I wish I could have been alone. Still, I know that Don is goodhearted, and after what we went through I consider him a friend. I try to compose myself. "Come sit down for a minute," I say to him, and we go into the main room. He sits on his bed, looking concerned, and I try to figure out how to start.

"Remember when we were outside Savannah and you asked what brought me to the streets?" I ask.

Don nods. "Yes, of course."

"I told you that I didn't know, and you mentioned that I say Renee's name when I sleep, and with that information I had a bit of a breakthrough."

"Yes, I remember."

I cough and continue. My voice and hands are shaky, but I look him in the eye as I speak. "When I first went to D.C., I didn't know what brought me there. I was in a muddled state of mind. Since that time, I've had two dreams that have helped reveal the past to me. I had the first one shortly after I got to the streets, and I didn't totally understand it at the time." I pause and look out the window, then look back at Don and tell him, "I just had the second one."

He looks confused and concerned, so I just spill it out. "Renee was my wife! She and our two children, Daniel and Prudence," I pause and take a deep breath, "were killed in a car crash." I wait before adding, "And I couldn't admit it to myself until now."

94

"My God, man," Don says. I see that he's genuinely concerned, but at a loss for what to do or say.

I look away. I don't know what else to say either. I'm not even sure how I'm feeling. I lower my head between my legs. I want him to leave. "I'll tell you more later," I finally say, and I take the twenty from Richardson out of my pocket and hand it to him. "You don't mind getting something for me?" I ask. "I need to be alone right now."

I see him noticing how badly my hand is shaking. "Of course not," he says, and he gives me a pat on the back. He stands over me for a moment before leaving—evaluating me, I suppose. Then he heads out the door.

I lay down. My heart is racing and I'm drenched with sweat, but I have to digest this, regardless of how numb and worn out I feel. I try to think. My hands clench into fists as I try to remember getting married to Renee or any experience thereafter that wasn't unveiled in the dreams. The calmness that I felt while talking to Don dissipates and I begin to panic, so I divert myself and begin to think of what we need to buy once we get a full paycheck: some new clothes, towels, work boots. Then I realize that I've run away from this disaster for too long— avoided it to the point where it became unrecognizable—and this time I have to face it.

I try to relax and focus. I begin the chronological sequence again, just as I had done outside Savannah, starting with my teenage days in Delaware. I remember the first time I saw Renee, and then I recall our walk along the beach and how we used to go into town and hang out at the diner. I grab my head with both hands. "What the fuck happened next?" I bellow. I pace back and forth by my bed, and stop as something comes to me. *College! The summer after our senior year, we decided we would go to college together. I know that I went to Maryland, but I just can't picture her being there with me.* I distinctly remember living in the house that was in the dream, and now I vaguely remember a baby crying there during the night. I recalled from the dream that his name was Daniel, but now that the dream is over, I again can't picture his face and all the clear images are again slipping away from me.

I feel very fucked-up, so I go outside, past the rows of housing with the running and hollering children and back towards the magnolia trees that border the plantation. My head is buzzing and long-lost realizations now bombard me from all directions. I think back to when I fled from the cottage and remember that Austin had told me that Renee and the children had been killed eighteen months ago that day. *There. That's what brought you to Washington.* I feel a brief sense of accomplishment for answering one of the haunting questions, but it's all coming too fast to embrace the victory. I move on and try to remember the crash. Vaguely, again, I can recall being alone at the house and seeing state troopers at the door, and my legs going out from under me and one of the cops supporting me as we walked to the sofa. I hadn't remembered that before, and I still feel other recollections swirling around in my head, waiting for their opening to come out. I feel overwhelmed and nauseous, and judgment tells me that I need to rest and digest this in small amounts. I take note of one item in particular, though— the fact that I'm not feeling any pain or sense of loss with this disclosure. Yes, I feel close to a breakdown from everything that's been unearthed, but I do not yet feel the pain. Maybe it's because I've yet to allow myself to remember how much I loved them, and without yet feeling it, I surely know that I did. That, I fear, will be the hardest part. That, I believe, is why my subconscious led me to bitter winter homelessness. I go back to the shack and lay on the bed until the shaking subsides and I go to sleep.

Several hours pass before Don comes back. The sound of

him taking the items he'd bought out of their bags and putting them into the refrigerator and cabinet wakes me. I sit up in bed, and once again I'm in the world I've come to know. I ask him how the town was. He tells me that it was good to him, and explains how he'd taken his share of the twenty and quadrupled it at the pool table of a local bar.

I get up and see what he's brought back. He's got some canned tuna, a loaf of bread, two packs of lunch meat, two packs of cigarettes, bar soap, canned beans, a saucepan, toilet paper, paper towels and a six-pack of Budweiser. "How much do I owe you?" I ask.

"Not a penny, my friend," he says sincerely and without a smile.

"Thanks," I say.

"How are you?" he asks.

"I'm doing better now. It'll just take some time."

He goes outside for a smoke, and a minute later I go out, too. He hands a cigarette to me—the once-a-week smoke that I've had since I met him. I light up and we walk down the trail and down to the dirt road that goes to the open fields. I check them out as we pass by and try to guess what we'll be doing. We continue on and come to a nineteenth-century style mansion, complete with pillars that span the length of the porch. The house is separated from the road by a white picket fence that's about chest high to us. Morris and his wife are sitting on a porch swing. I think about waving, but I'd gotten the impression that he didn't want to be bothered by his laborers. We turn and head back to our quarters.

Neither of us has a watch, so we take turns staying awake and keeping an eye for morning's break. It reminds me of the watches we'd take at our site in D.C. when we'd take shifts to keep the fire burning. We need to get an alarm clock with Friday's pay. I've slept during the day so I take the first shift, wondering what the next day will bring.

CHAPTER NINE

The official start to our workweek arrives at six-thirty. Richardson is at the door smoking a cigarette, waiting for us to pack the lunch he told us to make for the field. Don is hurriedly slapping sandwiches together and I look for the grocery bag to use as our lunch box. I glance back at Richardson and I can tell that we're trying his patients, but to our defense, he never had told us what time we'd be starting. I find the bag, Don stuffs the unwrapped sandwiches in it and we're off.

We follow Richardson down the dirt path and to the large open field. Already there's a gathering of what I'd guess to be fifty laborers, most of them Mexican, with a few blacks and whites sprinkled amongst them. In the field across the road is an equal sized assemblage already working. I nudge Don, nod toward the orange groves where we obviously won't be working and shrug my shoulders. Don raises his eyebrows in an I-don't-know-either manner as we go toward the edge of the field, where Richardson stops and turns to us. "Every year rocks get pushed up from underneath, then brought to the surface when we run the field cultivator through. We need to get'em out before we plant and we gotta do it by hand." He bends down and picks up one that's about the size of a baseball. "This is the size we're looking for. Anything this size or bigger. "If you want to have a smoke or stretch out your back do it now. You got about five minutes before Higgins gets here with the trailer." He starts to go, then stops and says, "What are your names again?"

"Carl," I say.

"Last name," he says. "We only go by last names here." Then adds, "Too many Juans and Ricos."

"Morgan," I say, and "Clay," Don says, and Richardson walks away and toward Morris' office.

"Clay?" I repeat to Don with a slight grin.

"Yes sir! Donald Clay at your service—stone picker extraordinaire."

Don has his morning cigarette as I survey our surroundings. All the Mexicans are gathered together while the rest of the workers are huddled in small groups. I stand alone and look down the field, which runs as far as I can see, and I wonder how long this seemingly-impossible job of clearing stones will take. I feel it's a hopeless task, but force myself to realize that people have done this before, so it must be achievable, and remind myself that I'll be getting paid to do it.

The sound of Higgins coming around the last bend in the dirt road marks the beginning of our workday. He positions the trailer about five yards ahead of us and the laborers spread out around it and commence with the stone picking. I ask the guy next to me, "How long do you think this will take?" He looks at me, then shrugs. The guy next to him says, "He no English." I nod at them and begin to pick up rocks and toss them into the trailer. I notice how most of the Mexicans are short, and I think about the advantage they have. I decide it'll be easier for me if I pick while kneeling. The ground is still somewhat damp from the rains they had two days earlier and the mud cakes to my pants. I add a cheap pair of jeans to my list of items to buy come payday.

We move along at a surprisingly good clip, and after an hour we've gone about fifty yards. Richardson stops by to check our progress and seems pleased, judging from his mannerisms, but still hollers out, "Come on! Let's get-a-movin'!" He checks again an hour later. We seem to be on an acceptable pace as this time he doesn't incite us, but rather announces a ten minute break. I slowly stand and stretch out my legs and back. Richardson stays and has a smoke with us, and when the break's over he tells me to follow him back to the barn.

"I'm gonna put'cha on water detail," he says as I trail him. We go into the barn and he hands me the keys to a four wheel off-road vehicle. On the passenger's seat are three two-and-a-half gallon water jugs. He picks one up and points to a garden hose in the corner. "Let it run till the water gets cold, then take these, rinse'em out good and fill'em up. There's a shelf over there," he points, "with Dixie cups and plastic bags for the trash. Make a run every two hours, but between runs, go back to pickin'. At the end of the day this gets parked right back where it is now."

Richardson leaves the barn and I get this process going. When I get to the field I start with Don, whom I haven't had much of a chance to talk with yet today. His brow is sweaty and his left arm is bleeding. "Tripped on a rock," he says as he sees me eyeing his wound. He downs three cups of water and I move onto the others. I notice a formality in this process as no one gathers around me; rather, they wait for me to go to them. I make a second trip to the barn to refill. I count the workers as I do this task and tally forty-seven, including my-self—thirty nine Mexicans, five white men and three blacks. I speak to a young kid named Wilson. He's quite loquacious, and he tells me a little about the place and the other workers. Apart from Don and me, only the Mexicans live in the housing units. The others are locals from Mount Dora. Wilson is quick to point out that they get an enhanced wage of six dollars an hour, seeing they're not getting the free housing. There'll be soybeans planted in the field that we're clearing. Last year they planted corn there, but they rotate crops so not to deplete the soil from all it's nutrients. Besides the orange groves, there are two other fields that we can't see from here. One already has watermelon in it and in the other they'll grow cotton.

The day wears on; the work is tedious and time goes by slowly. Don and I are out of shape, and by the two o'clock break it's showing on the both of us. My back aches, but I'm glad I've been assigned the water job, as it takes me out of the field for about twenty-five minutes after each break. Don found some English-speaking Mexicans who told him that it'll take two days to clear stones from this field, and then we'll move on to the other two fields. I wonder if it'll get better—if I'll get in shape or if I'll never get used to the wear and tear on my back and knees. And then there's the tedium. Picking rocks for twelve hours a day is a chore mentally. However, the day finally comes to an end and Don and I retreat to our shack.

I'm tired as hell and I want to crash, but I fight myself not to go to sleep too early. Don jests that it's my turn to cook and I make two more bologna sandwiches. I take another walk after we eat, back to the edge of the woods and camp under one of the magnolias. It feels good to relax and not think about anything. I look at the sky and see dark clouds coming in from the west. I look back toward the shack and see Don chatting with some of the Mexicans. I can see a difference in him already. This self reliance has given him a better outlook. I had never thought of him as a street bum anyway, as I had with the others. From the day I met him I sensed he had both the character and capabilities that went beyond that designation. Now I sense that he, like myself, is nurturing the seed of purpose, and, like myself, I wonder where he'll go from here.

I kill time until eight thirty, then go back to the shack. I can't stay awake any longer. Don had asked the man in the neighboring shack to give us a wake-up knock so we can both sleep through the night. I lay down and close my eyes, just as the rain begins to fall, bringing a melodic patter to the roof above. I see the rocks of the field in my head. I open my eyes in an attempt to disrupt the image, but they're back as soon as I close them. This goes on for an hour or so until I'm finally lulled to sleep by the soothing sound of the storm.

I don't awaken until I hear the knock signaling morning's arrival. Once I had finally nodded off, I had a perfect rest; the dreamless kind where you wake in the same position that you went to sleep in, and you doubt that you turned at all over the course of the night. I feel surprisingly refreshed and energetic, and I sit and stretch until Don introduces me to Luis, our neighbor. I slip my pants on and get up to shake his hand. He's a short fellow with oily looking hair and a sun-hardened face. He speaks accurate English, but rolls his R's with a dramatic flair. His hand feels hard and callused as I greet him. He speaks with pride about his two small sons after Don had asked him if he had a family, and he invites us to stop by some evening, but then prompts us to hurry, saying that Richardson does not accept tardiness. He heads for the field, while Don, again, fixes two sandwiches.

We get to the field and it's about eight furlongs of mud, beginning with where we stand and continuing on to where the ground crests into a small knoll. Richardson is standing in the middle of the field, as if to show that it is workable, and the mud rises past the tops of his work boots. He sees us, trudges through the quagmire to tell Don that he'll have water detail today. He then tells me, come first break, to go to the barn and show him what to do. I note the authority with which he speaks, not loud or overbearing, simply effective. I find myself respecting the fellow, despite the twenty years that I probably have on him. I have also noticed that he's very direct and unwavering with the Mexicans, yet they're the ones he chats and laughs with when he comes to the field to time our breaks.

I look up to the sky before stepping into the muddied work zone, hoping for a sign of an impending deluge that will cut our day short. There are fast-moving clouds overhead, but their shades of gray aren't dark enough to give any hope of anything imminent. I step into the cold mud and work my way towards Higgins and the trailer and the gathering of laborers around it. There are two new hires in the field today, local kids, Allan Beau and Johnny Bean, the latter of the two asks that he be called by both names. Allan looks unimpressive, or maybe uninspired, and quite ordinary. Johnny Bean is a fast talker, but he has character and I sense that he will keep things interesting around here. Don looks at the new kids and nods. "We' got some seniority already," he jests.

The topic runs its course and once again I feel the cold mud, which has now overrun my shoes and is seeping down my ankles and nestling at the soles of my feet. I grow eager for the first payday and hope I'll have money to spare for some work boots. As we make our way down the field, Allan comes up from behind and starts working alongside me. I don't say anything at first, but eventually acknowledge him with a nod.

"This sucks!" he says. "How long you been doin' this?"

I stand and straighten my back. "This is only my second day," I tell him.

"Man, I ain't cut out for this," he says with a growl. "Between all the mud and the niggers and all these fuckin' wetbacks... them people's made to do this shit, not us. You know what I'm sayin'?"

"Then why are you doing it?" I ask.

"Need the money, man, just like you. Now you can't tell me you work with these monkeys for the fun of it."

I don't respond, I just bend down and resume throwing rocks into the trailer, hoping that if I ignore him he'll go away.

"Now you ain't one of them nigger lovers, are ya?" he presses.

I stand straight again and look him in the eye. I may be disoriented but I'm not small and he's made a direct insult to the man who's become my best friend. "I think you'd better go pick over there somewhere," I point.

He doesn't leave. He steps forward and stands chin to chin with me. I don't want to start a fight—I would be screwed now if I were to be fired—but he has a shitty smile on his face and I do want to punch him. Yet, I hold off. Others begin to sense the imminence of a showdown. Then Richardson sees what's happening, runs over and thrusts himself between us.

"What the hell is going on here?" he yells.

I shake my head in disgust, not saying anything at first, but when Richardson presses I angrily blurt out, "This kid's a racists and he makes me sick. He insulted just about everyone here and expected me to agree with him."

Allan Beau doesn't argue. The belligerent bastard just continues to sneer. Richardson turns and gives him a one-handed shove in the direction of the road. "Get the fuck out of here," he says, then turns to the rest of the crowd and says, "Fun's over—everyone back to work." He waits until the kid is on the road and on his way out, then he, too, walks away. To my surprise, he has left me without reprimand. When the work day ends, Don and I are invited to go into town for some beers with a group of Mexicans. I explain how I'm low on cash at the moment, but they assure us that the drinks will be on them tonight. It seems like I made friends after the encounter with Allan Beau.

The first week passes and I begin to get acclimated with my new surroundings. With my first paycheck in almost two years I feel self-reliant and useful. I'm performing a task, however menial it may be, and I'm part of the production society. After the first payday I bought not only the food and supplies that I needed, but also the pair of boots, some new socks, a pair of jeans and some underwear. Don and I split the tab on an alarm clock, but perhaps the most important purchase I made was a pen and a journal. Now, as Don is sitting on Luis' front porch drinking a beer, I make my first entry and try to organize my thoughts.

By the end of the second week we have cleared the rocks out of three fields. Richardson has taken a liking to Don. I don't believe he dislikes me, but he doesn't speak to me unless it's about the job. Nonetheless, he treats me fairly, and I do whatever they ask of me. Johnny Bean has become the jokester of our work crew. It's all sophomoric stuff, but having someone there who keeps us on our toes makes the days interesting, and consequently, somewhat shorter. The other day he cut the tail off a dead raccoon, then snuck up behind Don and affixed it to the belt loophole on the back of his pants with a clothespin. All of us around Don laughed and we wouldn't tell him why, and it wasn't until the sun had descended from it's high noon position that he saw the tail's shadow and figured out that he had been played.

The more friends I make here the more I feel at home, and the more I feel at home and comfortable, the more personal progress I'm able to make. As with my other stops on this journey of self-analytical reconstructionism, I begin to develop a routine. At the cottage it was my visits to the diner, in Pennsylvania it was the walks down the country road, and in D.C. it was the pre-dawn walks through the city. Now, I find my peace in the magnolia trees that rim the field across from our quarters. After we finish our workday and grab a quick meal, Don heads over, beer in hand, to Luis' front porch, or vice versa, and I head to the edge of the woods with my journal. The first entries I made were merely organizational, but now I'm beginning to feel the sequence of which I must write. As I sit and make my tenth entry, I understand that the groundwork has been laid and the time for painful words to flow from my mind and onto this tablet of paper is near.

Another week goes by. We've been moved to the watermelon fields toward the back of the plantation and the work is excruciatingly hard. From dusk till dawn we lift eight to forty pound melons almost continuously. Richardson gives those who do this job a five minute break every hour, and an hour lunch to rest and recover, but the end of the day leaves my back aching and my spirit frail. Now, worn from this day, I retire an hour earlier than usual, even though it's a payday. Don has gone into town with Luis and the boys for the evening and the quarters are quiet, except for the sounds of the small Mexican voices that permeate the walls.

I close my eyes and again begin loading watermelon, a vision I see nightly now. Tonight I don't fight the replay as I usually would by distracting my mind with some strategic mental excercise. Tonight I succumb to the scene and keep loading until sleep comes. And when it finally does I am visited for the third time. This time there is no fog and there are no shadowy figures. It's Renee with the two children, one at each side of her. I slowly walk toward them and she wears a caring look but not a smile. "Carl, my father was right," she says. "It's time you face the fact that we were killed." I collapse to my knees, but she continues. "You've been running from our memory, but the love we have is greater than this tragedy." I look at her and try to tell her that the loss is too great, but I can't speak. "No, Carl," she continues. "There is no excuse for dismissing us from you memory. Pretending that the accident didn't happen doesn't change anything. The children and I are dead, but we need you to remember us. We need you to keep loving us." And then Renee, Daniel and Prudence slowly changed to translucent figures as Renee's last words echoed into a fade... "We need you to remember us. We need you to keep loving us. We need you to remember us. We need you to keep loving us."

I awaken and stare wide-eyed at the ceiling, but feeling clear-headed. I sit up, toss back the covers and pull my pants on. Oddly, I'm not shaken from the dream, but stranger than that, I realize that I now remember everything. I feel as sad as one should when filtered by two years of grieving. I feel acceptant of the tragedy, as though I had not gone into denial and time had begun to heal me. I picture Renee and the children standing before me, and when I do, I smile. In my thoughts I speak to them, saying what I wasn't able to in my dream:

It's so good to see you again, and it feels good to remember this part of my life. I love all of you so much. I look forward to the time I'll have alone where I can reflect upon our lives and the good times we shared. I had only dismissed you from my memory because I loved you so much and the reality was too brutal to accept. And for not tending to your memory, for not putting flowers on your graves, I am eternally sorrowful. I'm sure that things are looked upon differently wherever you're at and I'd guess that you don't suffer from embarrassment, but still, I apologize for becoming someone who's looked down upon by society. For your sakes only, I, your husband and your father, should not be looked down upon. I've brought shame upon myself, your representative on this earth, and for that which can not be undone I am remorseful. But yet, after two years without you in my life, I now feel as though you've been with me all along—and I'm sure that you have.

I open my eyes and I smile.

I see a pack of cigarettes on Don's nightstand and pop one out and grab the book of matches, then head to the front step. The night air is warm, the neighbor children are asleep and all is quiet. I'm glad that Don is out on the town and I can be alone. Still, I'm anxious to talk to him about the experience I've had and how all of a sudden everything is clear to me, but perhaps that conversation is best saved for the sobriety of morning. Besides, I need time to think of what to say. He assuredly thinks I'm at least half crazy anyway, and to blurt out, "I'm cured!" Well, there has to be a more subtle and explanative way. I go outside and have the cigarette, then, after staring at the sky in trance-like thought, I go back to bed.

I'm awakened Saturday morning by a flurry of sound, followed by a pounding on our door. I look at the clock: it's only 4:27. Don's still asleep and snoring over the commotion. I get up to answer. It's Luis. He comes in and shuts the door behind him. He sees Don sleeping and shakes his leg until he sits up and blurts out an expletive. "Sorry to wake you, man, but the feds are here on a crackdown and I got to hightail it, man."

"What?" Don says.

"Yeah, man, word is that that redneck kid who Richardson fired told someone that there were illegal migrants here. And I guess you can figure out now that I'm an illegal migrant. They're going around and taking everyone's social security numbers and if you don't have one then they're taking you away."

Don springs out of bed. "Where are they now?" he asks Luis.

"I don't know, man, but I got to go now."

"Wait one second, amigo," Don says. "I'm coming with you." He grabs two plastic grocery bags and takes whatever he can fit into them, then hurriedly dresses. He turns to Luis. "Give me fifteen seconds to say goodbye," he tells him, and Luis nervously looks out the door and steps outside, telling Don to hurry. Everything is happening so quickly that it doesn't seem real, yet here is my closest friend about to tell me farewell.

"I hate to do this so quickly, Carl, but I guess this is goodbye. You understand that I can't tell you my real name. And because of that you won't be able to look me up, so we'll never see each other again." His voice is crackling, but he goes on. "I've enjoyed your company and I wish you the best, man." He puts one arm around me and gives me a half-hug as he holds the two bags in the other hand. I do the same.

There's so much I want to tell him. He's the only one who'd understand the importance of the dream I had, and consequently the only one worth mentioning it to, and I want to talk about it so badly. Yet, I understand the urgency of the situation. "And all the best to you," I say instead. "And be safe."

And he turns and rushes out the door.

And just like that, I am alone.

Time passes again as it always does and eventually I get used to not having Don around. Yet I think about him often and wonder how he's doing. But the new roommate they have sharing quarters with me is quiet and keeps to himself, so the situation is acceptable. Although he too is Mexican, he goes by Robert—not Roberto. The solitude I have lets me reflect on things, such as the friendship I had formed with Don and the experiences we shared. But mostly I think about Renee and our children and try to understand how I came to think so clearly so suddenly. I know it was just a dream that snapped me into reality, but I feel as though Renee had actually spoken to me, chastised me and encouraged me. Yet, I try to understand how the quagmire I was in was ultimately dissolved so quickly.

During the raid we had lost seventeen migrant workers and Don. Three other workers, including Johnny Bean, quit before more workers were hired because of the increased work burden that was tossed upon those of us who remained.

I have now been at the plantation for more than two months. It's a Sunday morning in early April and the Florida weather has nearly reached perfection. The months I've spent in the various fields have put me in the best physical condition of my life, but moreover, the confidence I've gained from putting all the pieces of the past together makes me feel that I'm ready for the world again. I'm sitting on the ground leaning against our shack, thinking about what I always think about lately—how to assimilate back into society—when a black Lincoln comes down the dirt drive. The car is unfamiliar and the windows are tinted, and I wonder who's inside and what kind of trouble I may have gotten into. It pulls up in front of the shack and the door flies open. A peaceful smile comes to me as I see the familiar face. "Carl! Carl! It's you! I can't believe I finally found you!"

It's Julia. She's crying and laughing and she drops to her knees and wraps her arms around me, swaying back and forth as she hugs me. I try to look at her, but she's overwhelming, and in my sitting position I can do nothing but wait for her to relent. Finally, she leans back. "Julia," I say. And I smile. My nature is casual and relaxed and my lack of excitement brings worry to her face, so I take her forearm and gently say, "I'm okay now. I've found my answers—and my peace."

She begins to ask a series of questions, not waiting for an answer before going on to the next one. I hold my palm up and ask her to slow down. She takes a breath and composes herself, then asks, "What happened after you left the cottage?"

"I assume you've talked to Austin," I say, but knowing it was a needless question.

"Of course," she says, then takes a breath, still in apparent disbelief that she located her long-lost brother. "He called me right after you stormed away. And he's been worried sick about you."

I sit up straight and clear my throat, while Julia shifts into a cross-legged sitting position. "Let me start by saying that this plantation saved me," I say as I turn and point toward the fields of newly planted corn that lay to my left and continue on as far as we can see from our vantage point. "The streets of Washington D.C. saved me. As brutal as they were, they kept me from putting a bullet in my head. I guess that's what I needed at the time—brutality. The streets were so bitterly cold that all I could think about was how I could get warm. Consequently, I found inside of me a will to survive."

I look up at Julia and she looks puzzled at the mention of D.C., so I tell her everything in sequential order; some of what I told her she had known even when I didn't, the rest of what I said helped her understand why I acted the way I did—and that I would now be okay. I begin with Henry Olafson's farm, and then to the streets of Washington.

"Whenever the weather eased and I didn't need my mental energy to stay warm, I'd try to recall what had happened the day I left the cottage. Even though my thinking wasn't clear, I knew that answers to the past were the key to the future, and the key to the future would begin by unlocking one particular day. So I trudged through these layers of mental obstacles that were burying my memories of the accident, and everything that was subsequent. I got only glimpses of them at first, but with Renee's help, they gradually became more and more clear."

Julia furrows her brow, suddenly looking worried again. I explain myself.

"During the time I was away, I had a series of dreams. I had the first one in D.C. and the last two here. The first one confused me, but it made me want to know what had happened—what could have been so horrible that I would abandon my home and live in such a bitter environment. As I reflected upon it, I had some recollections—vague at first, but the more I contemplated, the more I realized that there was a reality that I wasn't facing. So I'd think about the dream's contents until I got so scared or depressed that I wanted to kill myself. Then I'd back off and become distracted again by the harshness of the streets." I chuckle. "Ironic, isn't it? The harshness of homelessness kept me alive."

Julia smiles; her expression shows that she's struggling to comprehend. I smile to reassure her, although I still haven't found ease in talking about what I had to say next.

"When I finally figured out that Renee, Daniel and Prudence had been killed, I realized it in a matter-of-fact way. It was, at that point, simply an answer to why I'd been acting the way I was. I felt no emotion. My wife and kids were dead. Problem solved. Still, I knew that I had and would feel something eventually, but for the time being, I let the truth slip back into the distant echelons of my mind. But by grand design or instinct, whichever you believe in, either God or nature gave me my answers in small doses; I couldn't have handled it any other way."

Then I tell Julia about the third dream and how Renee had essentially ordered me to get back on life's track. I told her how real the dream seemed, and I told her how it ended, with Renee repeating, "We need you to remember us. We need you to keep loving us." My voice cracks with the last two sentences and my throat tightens, but for the first time since the accident I'm in the presence of someone I can cry with while being fully aware. So with my sister at my side—someone who actually knew Renee, Daniel, and Prudence—I let it all out.

CHAPTER TEN

As I sit in back alone on the ride back to Virginia, I recall the love I had with Renee and the life we shared—every little detail and nuance of it. I think of how in the harshest of settings, the past slowly came to me. By instinct I had fled from the familiarity of Virginia and Delaware, seeking relief from a turmoil that I wasn't prepared to handle. Henry Olafson's farm was a safehouse for me. It was geographically removed from places that prompted horrific memories, and a place where the healing could begin at the slow pace that was needed. Next, I needed preparation for the most brutal of cruelties. Without comprehension or knowledge of intent, I went to the streets of D.C.—my surroundings had to be as harsh as the revelations that were about to come. And by that same instinct I migrated to Florida when I was ready to accept realities that were even more severe. But my recollections came in small portions—I don't know if I could have handled it otherwise—but when my memories were complete, I felt an inner peace. Now, as I have ample time on this journey home, I close my eyes and reflect upon the life I had.

After spending time together at our cottages in the summers of '71, '74 and '75, Renee and I attended the University of Maryland, with her getting a master's in business and me getting one in history. We were married in our junior year. We graduated from college and I was offered a teaching job in Burlington, Vermont. It wasn't anything special, just a high school position, but Renee and I fell in love with the city and it's wonderful location on Lake Champlain. So I took the job and we rented a small second-floor downtown apartment. Although the place itself was humble, the view of the lake from our balcony was spectacular.

We became social butterflies in those early days in Burlington. On weekends we'd hit the hottest clubs in the city and stay out till they closed, then crash the after-hours parties, often staying out until the sun rose. We met a lot of people and we were living on the fast track. We had both grown up clean, marijuana was the only drug we had dabbled in, but the lifestyle we were living introduced us to cocaine. Soon, the routine expanded from weekends only to five nights a week. The altruistic visions we had as teenagers, such as saving the planet from pollution and traveling to foreign lands with the Peace Corps, had been overwhelmed by the high we were on. We were a popular couple and we felt a freedom that neither of us had experienced. The mornings came early, but we never missed work, as tired as we might have been. However, an estrangement was forming between Renee and I whenever we were away from the crowd.

So we were doing lines and drinking and smoking—a far cry from the idealistic plans of our youth. After a year of this we began to burn out. It wasn't us; wasn't where we were from. We both felt the need to step away from the scene and get serious about our careers, and get back to the qualities that made us fall in love. We evolved from fun-loving post-college kids, to young adults who discovered that their time had come to take what the world had to offer. So we tightened our belts and began to build for the future.

When we first came to Burlington, Renee had taken a sec-retarial job. It was rather low paying, but she liked her boss and fellow employees. But with our recommitment, she took an-other look at what was available and found a better paying secretarial position. I began looking to the next level as well. We moved out of our overpriced downtown apartment and found a place on the outskirts of the city. I interviewed for a position at the University of Vermont. I was in the final small group of candidates, but they hired a retiree who had previ-ously taught at Rhode Island. The following spring, he died, and I was hired as a history professor.

I loved the job and in a short time I became very good at it. I was avant-garde in a field of full professors who taught in traditional ways. I became interactive with my classes; I rolled my sleeves and loosened my tie and challenged my students to think. I'd often ask them, after discussing a certain time in his-tory, to find the closest present-day scenario to that event. I sometimes got myself in trouble, but I always seemed to have the full attention of my students and they enjoyed being in my classes.

The next several years were productive for us. We both worked hard and put in a lot of hours and we were seeing the benefits of our labor. Our bank account was healthy, but we hardly had time for one another. Except for occasional trips to Virginia and Maryland to visit parents, we hadn't taken a vaca-tion in the nine years we were in Vermont. So, at the end of the summer of 1990 we took a trip to Martha's Vineyard. It was great being someplace new, and Renee and I experienced a much-needed renaissance. Six weeks later we found out that she was pregnant, and in the spring of 1991, she gave me a son.

Daniel brought us closer together. He was a very happy child; he hardly ever cried and always smiled when we spoke to him. I was so proud. He would be my legacy—the Morgan whose loins would take our name into the twenty-first century. I had so much planned for him, even though he was just an infant, and I was prepared to do anything to make sure he had everything good in life. Renee had quit her job and concentrated on raising our son, and I saw her in a new light. It was funny how the girl I had known for so long could have had this other dimension—the much-talked-about maternal instinct—she seemed to know the hows and whys without anyone having to tell her. Then, twenty-two months later, in the spring of '93, our daughter was born.

Prudence was a serious child. She wasn't fussy or moody, but even as a baby, she wore an expression of introspection and contemplation, as though she was already trying to figure out what the world was all about. In fact, I recall trying to call her Pruddy, but the nickname didn't fit a child with such a solemn look. Daniel was jealous, of course, and Renee gave him extra attention. Consequently, he became Mama's boy and Prudence became Daddy's girl.

We stayed in Vermont for another two years. The kids were growing fast and Renee longed for them to be closer to their grandparents, so in the summer of 1995 we moved to Manassas, Virginia. There, we were located almost halfway between my parents in Fredericksburg, and Austin and Gertrude, who were in Germantown, Maryland. Renee was ready to get out of the house, and she took a secretarial job for an accounting firm. I couldn't find work for several months, but we had enough bankrolled to get us through on one income and I enjoyed being home with the kids.

Every other weekend we'd visit the grandparents, alternating the visits between my parents and hers. Daniel was old enough to look forward to the trips, while Prudence was content to go wherever we would take her. I enjoyed going to

Germantown as much as Renee and Daniel did. Austin and Gertrude loved to see the kids and were the quintessential grandparents. Austin and I would take Daniel on Saturday mornings and go to the farmer's market, while the girls would stay at the house and make desserts, go to yard sales, or visit Renee's relatives. During those days, Austin became a second father to me. I enjoyed his colloquial way of speaking and listening to his old-world wisdom. Gertrude, on the other hand, never seemed to notice that I was no longer the teenager who was dating her daughter. She thought that I lacked the knowledge to care for her daughter and grandchildren, and constantly pointed out the simplest of things to me as though I'd been oblivious to them. I guess in that way, she was the quintessential mother-in-law. Despite her lack of faith in me, I was saddened when she died of a heart attack, just one year after we had moved to be closer to them. I felt so bad for Austin. Although he tried to be stoic, he seemed lost and very alone. We made extra trips to Germantown during that time, trying to lift his spirits and giving him extra time with his grandchildren.

Sadness continued to visit us over the next two years. My mother was taken in the winter of '96. A short five months later my dad died. It was so strange losing both of my parents in such a short span. I felt bad for the children, too. They had gone from having four grandparents to one, and even though they were too young to understand what they were missing out on, I felt bad that they wouldn't have all that love and influence throughout their childhood.

Daniel and Prudence grew quickly, both physically and intellectually. In no time, they were enrolled in school and had their own little friends and their own personalities. Daniel was active and outgoing, while Prudence was reserved and rather sophisticated for a six year-old. In that time, the influence that Renee and I had with the children was transposed—Daniel was now Daddy's boy and Prudence became Mom's girl. Still, I loved both of my children equally, in a way that only parents understand.

So it comes to the cold, hard conclusion of my recollections—that day, a little more than two years ago—their last day with me. It was Tuesday, the fifth of March, 2002. There was a storm that hit Manassas that day. We had gotten about an inch and a half of rain, but as the evening progressed and the temperatures plummeted, the roads began to ice, but it was a black ice—the ice that forms in patches that are undetectable until you come upon them. Renee had to go to the drug store, which meant getting on 28, which is an undivided highway. The kids had been restless that evening and wanted to go with their mother, and I had papers to correct and didn't mind the thought of having some quiet time, so I didn't object, even though it was a school night. They hadn't made it far at all, less than a mile from the house, when Renee hit a patch of ice and lost control of our minivan. She slid into an oncoming vehicle. Renee and Daniel were killed instantly. Prudence died while the paramedics were tending to her. The couple in the other vehicle came out unscathed.

I had heard the ambulance go by, as we were just a few blocks off the highway, and for a fleeting second I'd wondered if anything could have happened to Renee or the kids. But I dismissed it, as we all have to when we over-worry, and went back to correcting my papers. I was so involved that I hadn't noticed that an hour had gone by—going to the drugstore is a fifteen minute endeavor at best—but when I heard the doorbell ring I had an eerie feeling. I reluctantly opened the door, and upon seeing the state troopers my heart dropped out of my chest. I collapsed onto the floor in grief. They helped me to the sofa and let me compose myself some, but made me go to identify the bodies. I don't know if I would have lost my mind if I hadn't had to do that, but seeing the lifeless bodies... seeing your whole history and reason for existing laying dead in front of you... their bodies bloodied... I wasn't able to handle it.

From there I remember going in and out of coherence. The troopers took me home and asked if I'd be okay, and when I said that I would I was already going into denial. It was back and forth that whole night. I remember wailing with grief, and then the wails turned to sobs and sniffles, and soon I had the television on and was watching the Knicks play the Lakers on the Tuesday night game of the week. It continued to go like that until Julia and Jim arrived. Julia was obviously shocked and saddened, but she was also concerned about me, and with this I wasn't able to escape the tragedy anymore. It was then that my subconscious took over and I began my two-year hiatus from the truth.

Renee had warmed the earth with her beauty, both physical and social, for forty-three years. To say that she was the most beautiful woman on the planet, I suppose, would be hyperbole, but she was, nonetheless, in my eyes and in the eyes of my children. Her beauty came to me in many ways, be it the way she couldn't pass a beggar without giving him something, or the way her voice sounded when she sang in church, or how her mangled, morning hair made her look even more appealing, or the mole on the side of her right breast, or the way she could manage the kids when they were rambunctious. Renee had a natural way with everyone, regardless of their appearance or social standing, and everyone seemed to love her, and there will be a void in the world without her.

Daniel was a month shy of eleven when he died. I cry when I think of the enthusiastic way that my son approached life. Everything was incredible to him and the world was full of places to be explored and people to meet. Ironically, for as much as he wanted to do, I believe that if he could have been forewarned, death would have bothered him the least. He was happy-go-lucky, but took things as they came to him and he always seemed satisfied with what he had. I think about the joy we felt when he was born. I think of the fun I had doing traditional father-son things, like teaching him to ride a bike and throw a football.

Prudence is the one for whom I feel the most sorrow. She would have done great things, I have no doubt about that. She had her mother's compassion and an agenda that seemed already set, even though she was only nine. She was a beautiful child. I say beautiful because, from the time she was a baby, she seemed too sophisticated for the word cute. Yet, for as beautiful and benevolent as she was, she seemed scripted for a tragic life. She was my little darling and my little hugger—long solemn hugs, as if with each hug she was telling me that everything would be okay. The world is a lesser place with her untimely demise.

Lately, I spend a lot of time thinking about everything. I go for walks in secluded places and look at the trees and the clouds, and smell the grass and the leaves, and I think, and I observe. I observe that the clouds are not as white as they used to be, nor is the sky quite as blue—and they will never again be as splendid as they were. Yet, I wonder if not for the existence of Renee, Daniel and Prudence, could the clouds and the sky and the grass and the trees ever have been even as glorious as they are now. But I've come to realize that they are still the sky and the clouds and the grass and the trees, and they nonetheless feed my soul. They are evidence of God, and hence, evidence of the eternal existence of what I love. It is in that vast greatness that I find solace and comfort, and from that solace, I find that I'm able to go on.

CHAPTER ELEVEN

A sense of normalcy is beginning to return to my life. After staying with Julia for several days, she insists that it's best that I go back to the cottage. From what I told her, she says that it's where I should be, and I feel good about it too—especially that I'll be staying at a place that is half mine and that I won't be imposing on anyone, except for the need to borrow Julia's second car. The day after we got back to Virginia, she took me to the mall and bought enough clothes for me to restart my life with. I pack them into a small suitcase that belongs to Jim.

I'm anxious to get to Delaware. I feel like an interruption here, even though everyone has been nice to me. I need to be alone again to make the last phase of my transition to normalcy. I've recalled everything, and I've experienced the anger, pain and depression, although quite differently than most people would have, had they been in my situation. I may eventually date, but I'll probably never marry or have kids again. I have no desire to. It would be a betrayal to Renee, Daniel and Prudence. Still, I have to live out my life and I want each day to be better. I need to become societal again and get to the point where I find something in interactions with other people. I want to go back to the North Shores Diner. The locals are friendly to those who have connections there, and they've always been welcoming to me. I envision going in for breakfast, sitting at the counter reading the newspaper and commenting on the events of the day to the person next to me. Simple as it sounds, that would be one of my goals.

As I'm preparing for my departure, Julia comes into the spare bedroom where I've been staying. "How are you, Carl?" she asks.

I smile, close the suitcase and sit on the edge of the bed. "I'm good, Julia," I tell her.

"There's more that you need to know," she says, but she wears a gentle smile, so I know that this news won't be brutal. She sits next to me. "After you fled the cottage, in absentia, you failed a competency hearing and the court appointed me your administrator."

I sit patiently, thinking how humbling it is that my kid sister has this supervisory role over me. I wait for her to continue, but she is hesitant. "Jule, whatever it is, I'm ready," I say.

"I know," she says, "I just want to say this the right way." She looks out the window, then turns back and places her hand on my shoulder. "After what you've been through... I don't know how anybody can put a price on..." She pauses and looks down, then back at me. "Carl, I don't know how to say this."

"I have insurance money," I say for her.

She sighs. "Yes, Carl, you have a substantial sum that has been placed in an account for you."

It's my turn to look out the window. *How can you put a price on a life? Especially when it's someone you love?*

"I know you don't want to struggle with this now, but I have to let you know."

I stand and walk to the window that I've been staring through. I look out at a child riding her bike down the sidewalk, then turn back to Julia. "Thanks for telling me. I'd like to be alone now."

"In a minute, Carl," she says. "But we need to finish this

conversation. You need to know where you stand. You still haven't been declared competent, so that needs to be done. And as I said, the amount you have coming is substantial. Are you well enough to be responsible with it?"

I nod yes and she says, "All right, I'll let you be alone." Apparently, I haven't convinced her that the total recollection of the tragedy has brought me back to being a sane, albeit sad person. Then again, I knew that it would take time to regain everyone's trust in the fact that I can take care of myself. I go back to the window and resume watching the little girl ride her bike up and down the block, and my thoughts go to Prudence, then to Daniel, and finally Renee. They would all understand that I would give up the insurance money along with every-thing else I ever had if only they could return to me. But they can't. Still, how can you take a sum of money from someone who is basically saying, *Here, this is in exchange for your loved ones.* But what happened was God's will, not mine.

I spend the rest of the day killing time. I had taken a long walk in the early afternoon, and later played several games of horse with Julia's twelve year-old son. Now I sit with her fam-ily and watch sitcoms, occupying my time more than enter-taining myself.

Wednesday morning arrives and I go into the kitchen and have coffee and a light breakfast. When we finish eating, Jim and the kids run off in their separate directions, leaving me alone with my sister. I know she wants to polish off our con-versation from the night before. I get up and bring my plate to the sink and rinse it. "Come back and sit down," she says, and I return to the table. She's gauging me again, but I've spent most of the night dealing with the guilt of getting money for the deaths of people I love. I realize that insurance claims are a part of our society, and though there'll be no thrill in having this money, and I won't buy anything superfluous with it, I know that I have to take stewardship of it.

She addresses the matter in a businesslike way this time. "After Austin called and told us what had happened, we searched everywhere for you. The first thing I did was drive to your house, but you weren't there. After several weeks of not finding you, I realized that your bills weren't being paid and that you'd be in danger of losing your home. I knew that you had insurance money that you never came to terms with, so I went to the courts. They approved my oversight of your funds, and you had a generous settlement, Carl, so I paid off your house, your car, and all your credit cards."

"Thank you," I say.

She continues. "But we were still worried about you and had no clue where you were, so I hired the private detective."

Now I sit and look guilty, like an adolescent who just did something stupid.

"Anyway, Carl, at some point we have to go to court and have you declared competent to manage your funds."

Declared competent, I think. And suddenly I feel that feeling like a stupid adolescent wasn't so bad.

"There's something else, too. Something that Jim and I talked about on the first night you were here."

I wonder what this will be, but she looks calmer. She takes another drink of coffee, as if that were her buffer between topics, then continues.

"We know what the cottage has come to mean to you, and we don't want you to feel like you have to share it with us. We have enough money to get a vacation house of our own, and you have enough to buy out our half of the cottage."

"But what about your memories?" I ask.

She chuckles for the first time in four days. "Well, I'm assuming that you'll invite us there once in a while."

I smile too. And it sounds good. I like the idea of having

the cottage to myself without worry of intervention, even though that's not what Dad envisioned when he wrote his will. But then again, he couldn't have foreseen the catastrophe with Renee and the kids, and with that, how therapeutic this piece of property has been for me. I tell Julia that we'll get the cottage appraised and that we have a deal. We get up and I help her with the dishes.

She makes a call to the county building and tells me that the judge has agreed to see us ten minutes before noon. I tie up all my loose ends. The little I have is packed and at the foot of the bed. I tighten a necktie and check myself in the mirror as we prepare to go to the courthouse. I rehearse my lines in my head on the way there. Another item that's been restored is my pride, and for as much as I love Julia, I no longer want her to have authority over me.

I deliver a convincing testimony as to why I should be declared competent. The reason I fell into the previous state is obvious and I don't dwell on that. Nor do I mention how my clarity of thinking came from a dream—I thought such a statement would do more harm than good. Instead, I detail the chronology of my escapism and how each new venue brought me a step closer to facing such a devastating personal tragedy. The judge accepts my petition and I regain the status of a competent and viable person.

Now everything is done and I'm ready to delve into my new life. With my visit to Delaware imminent, I'm glad that the detective Julia hired found me when he did. I have no doubt that I would have eventually made it back to Virginia from Florida, had I been left to my own initiative, but kudos to her for making it happen all the sooner. For as much as I missed Don when he made his abrupt departure, little did I know that the registration of employee's social security numbers would be the catalyst for making my whereabouts known to my loving sister.

The summer sun beats down on my brow as the family gathers on the porch to wish me well. I throw the suitcase in the trunk and climb in the blue Mustang convertible, then back out of the driveway and wave one last time. Julia has such a cozy family, and I'm glad that the kids are home for their lunch hour to see me off. The family treats me well, although I sense that Jim's loss of respect for me is irrevocable. I pull onto the highway, turn on the radio and scan through the stations until I find the Oriole game. It's April thirteenth and this is the first game I've listened to since the week before last Labor Day and it sounds good to hear baseball again. I think back to the days of my youth and how I rooted for Paul Blair and Don Buford, Brooks Robinson and Boog Powell, and I find myself unfamiliar with any of the current players. Still, I realize that the game helps pass the time. As I drive I try not to think about how my reputation has been damaged from living as a street bum and not to wonder if the damage is irreversible, like I believe it is with Jim. Yet, these thoughts pepper me as I try to focus on the game. I turn the radio up a hair and scan my surroundings, looking for a diversion. My mind rests as I realize that better things wait ahead, and that they will continue to get better from now on. I know it'll take a while for me to reestablish myself and have my so-called recovery be as complete as possible, and, just as before, I believe the cottage will be a catalyst for that.

After several hours I find myself on familiar roads—Highway 7 to southbound Highway 1. The sun is high in the sky and I'm driving with all the windows open. The breeze awakens my senses and the stimulation begets me to plan what I can accomplish while I'm at the cottage. I have to finish up some details from the last time I was out there, and perhaps I can do some work on the inside as well. It'll be good for me to do something productive, as well as get back into a routine instead of just trying to survive. I have to put the experiences of Washington D.C. behind me and not let the embarrassment of being in such a humbling situation haunt me for the rest of my life. I have to win the trust of the North Shores residents with whom I will become close. And conversely, I have to accept the fact that some of them will never see me as normal, but eternally as the guy who flipped out and became a vagrant bum. But as I drive I appreciate the fact that my thoughts are no longer cluttered and that I feel whole again.

I get on the final stretch of road and I don't stop until I get to the cottage. It's dusk when I arrive. Before unlocking the cabin and unloading my gear, I take a walk over the dunes and to the sea. It's windy and the air smells saltier than usual and my senses are enlightened. I turn and look toward Austin's. There's a light on so I know he's up, which makes me feel good—any familiarity makes me feel good now. I'm anxious to see him, but the day has been long and I chose to make that encounter after a good night's sleep.

I turn and look southward down the shore as I think about the dream I'd had on my first night of homelessness. I've since come to realize how many people care about me, but it was my only lover, Renee, who gave me the reason and the will to survive. I go back to the cottage, unload and settle in for the night.

The next morning I take a look around. The paint job looks good. I truthfully didn't know what to expect, considering the state of mind I was in when I did the job. However, I still need to paint the trim, the eves and the window frames. The sky is clear and it's a good day for it. I see, too, that the storage shed is being overcome by weeds and saplings. I add that to my list of things to do.

Once I have my agenda set, I take a walk down the path. I

knock on the door several times before Austin answers. "Carl," he says. His voice is warm, but I can tell I've awakened him. He looks to be about three years older, although it hasn't yet been a year since I've last seen him. He seems to be gauging me—hesitant to ask anything—and though I'm willing to tell him everything that I've been through and all the doors that have been reopened, I don't want to get into that conversation just yet; I'm too anxious to dig into my projects. Instead, I say, "I'm all right now, Austin," and tell him that I'll fill him in on all the details, but that I want to get going on the cottage. I apologize for everything related to my abrupt departure of Labor Day Weekend. He understands, as I knew he would. I tell him what he means to me and he hugs me. Then, with all the formalities covered, we sit and have a cup of coffee.

I can't remember feeling so at peace as I did right then and there, in the wooden cabin made of pine, built long enough ago to be genuinely quaint, looking out past the dunes, with their grasses dancing to the cadence of the wind and toward the sea, and Austin, a humble old man in a flannel shirt, sitting across from me. I feel Renee's warmth through her father's eyes as he tells me that he's finished his repairs on the boat. I hear the sound of paws on the hardwood floor and see Tipi, looking just as sleepy as Austin, walking into the room. I feel a rush of joy as I see that the little guy's still alive. He goes to the old man, and as he rubs the dog's head, he says, "Don't you remember Carl?" Tipi looks at me as if he understands English. He, too, looks older and isn't as uppity. He saunters over and looks at me. "Hey there, buddy," I say. "It's good to see you, my little friend."

"Want to take him with you?" Austin asks.

I pat my leg and he jumps on my lap. "Yeah," I say. "I do."

Austin and I catch up on the small, general things, then I go back to the cottage and begin to put the finishing touches on what I'd done last summer. It seems like years ago and in a different world to me now, and I wouldn't want to go back to that time in my life, but I appreciate that summer for what it was. I know that that whole year was a chain of events, linked in necessary sequence. The time I spent working on the cottage began to clear my head and get me organized, and it forced my thinking to be purposeful. The time I spent in North Shores forced me to deal with people again. The tragic words of Austin temporarily unleashed everything that I had blocked out after the accident. Pennsylvania was a buffer zone placed between the harshness of the past and the severity yet to come. It was a mental sabbatical, a chance for me to recharge my life forces before taking the next unbeknownst step. The time on the streets put me in a condition where I could accept those bitter subconscious truths, and the harshness of the streets themselves, and the fact that I was surviving on them, gave me the fortitude and will to want to know what had happened. And finally, the fields of Florida were where everything came back to me. As humble as my job was and my accommodations were, it was an upgraded state of living for me, and with that, I was ready to upgrade myself back to living a normal life, and with that desire, I was willing to deal with all the ghosts of the past.

It's twilight when I drop my tasks and walk down to the boathouse. The sky is still blue, but a crescent moon is out, barely visible in the lighted sky, as if it itself were a ghost. I pat Austin on the back as we walk side by side to the ocean. If not for him saying what he did, I wonder where I might be right now. The time is right and I begin filling him in on what happened after I left the cottage—the day that would change my life—first to a living nightmare, but gradually into a normalcy that I hadn't previously been able to hope for. I look out over the sea. I see that his boat is out and tied to the dock. I turn to him, take a deep breath of the salty sea air, and with my arm hung around his shoulder I say, "It would be a good evening for a sail."

We head out onto the ocean and I get him caught up on everything. His eyes mist when I speak of Renee and the children, but he maintains composure and tells me, "You should write a book about all you've been through."

I smile softly. "What would I call it?"

He looks up at the ghostly body in the sky. "How about, *Falling From the Moon?*"

I smile again, close my eyes and listen to the waves splash against the boat.

CHAPTER TWELVE

After a full day of leisure, relaxation and companionship with Austin, I wake up eager to dig into my chores. I've also noticed that the temporary fix I had put on the roof last year has served its purpose, but it probably won't last much longer. I decide to put a new roof on the cottage. I drive into North Shores, stop at the waste disposal company and order a dumpster. Then I go to the lumber yard and order the nails, shingles, and the ice-and-water shield. They say they'll deliver it late morning or early afternoon, so I have time to stop into the diner, which is something I've been both anticipating and dreading. I realize that there'll be whispers about the crazy guy who knocked down his elderly father-in-law and stormed off. Perhaps some of them know more, like how I spent the previous winter as a street bum. And then there's the issue of facing Molly. To say that I didn't care what the other people thought wouldn't be true, but I could blow off any negative opinion that they might have of me. But I don't want to see a look of pity, disappointment or fear on Molly's face. Yet, it's the last challenge I have relating to my ominous disappearance of last year.

There's a stir of chitchat as I walk in, which, as luck would have it, seems to subside after a few patrons see that I've entered. I spot an unoccupied stool at the counter and head for it, making an effort not to avoid eye contact, but rather looking around and casually nodding as I do. It's killing me and I want to run out and never enter the place again, but I fabricate a smile as I sit and pull a newspaper in front of me. A waitress that I haven't seen before takes my order of coffee and a bagel, and as she leaves I force myself to turn my head and look for Molly. It would be so easy for me to live the rest of my life as a hermit, but I have committed myself to making the best of things, which means making my best attempt at everything—in this case, social interaction. When the waitress returns I ask if Molly still works at the restaurant. She says yes, but tells me she's off today. Fair enough; one conquest at a time.

I read the morning paper until I finish my coffee, then, after a stop at the gas station, I head for the cottage. I want to get the housework caught up before I begin working on the roof. The temperature has risen slightly and it should be a fair enough day for my project. I place the ladder at the back of the building, and with a cup of coffee in hand, I climb to the peak of the roof, sit and look out over the ocean. As soon as my supplies arrive I'll begin this job, but for now I'll appreciate the view from this vantage point. In a few ways I'm excited about my future. I have no pressure to retake employment; financially, I have no needs. Whether I will or not depends solely upon my desire. Rather, I look forward to enjoying moments like this one, overlooking the sea from the roof of my cottage. It is simple and non-extravagant, and for the sake of my loved ones, it's extravagance that I intend to avoid. I feel that enjoying such things as the innocent beauty beheld in nature would better serve their memory.

The flatbed truck arrives a little before noon and unloads my supplies, and the dumpster comes a short while later. Now I can begin. It feels good to do something constructive again.

I'm thankful that Don and I went to Florida. That gave me a taste of accomplishing seemingly impossible tasks, not to mention the fact that it got me into good physical shape. As I tear off shingles and frisbee them toward the dumpster below, I wonder what has happened to my friend. I hope that he's landed on his feet and is doing something that he enjoys. I also hope that someday he can confront the issue from his past and make himself eligible to live up to his potential.

After several hours on the job, Austin stops by. He climbs the ladder high enough to where he can see me, but doesn't come onto the roof. He asks if I'm hungry, I tell him I am, and he goes inside and fixes a meal. When it's ready I take my first break of the day and join him on the steps in front of the cottage. "I think my next project is to build a picnic table," I tell him.

He pats me on the back. "Now that's one I can help you with, but you won't catch me up there," he chuckles.

I take a bite of the barbecued beef sandwich and look up at the skies. They are still as blue and clear as they were earlier. I need to keep an eye on them, though. Once I begin pulling boards off I'll be at a point of no return. I'll have to tear them off and replace them with plywood all in the same day. With that done, though, I can always tarp the roof at the sign of rain.

Tipi comes sauntering out of the cottage and I get a kick when Austin refers to him as a lazy old man. Tipi, as if on cue, yawns and rolls over onto his side. I draw a parallel between the dog and myself. Whereas he lazes with age, I, too, feel that my best years are behind me, albeit for different reasons. Still, I've made it my mission not to give up on life and to seek the best in it.

With lunch behind me I begin to get into a rhythm. It's near dusk when I have all the shingles pulled and the tarpaper torn off. My back's a little sore, but not as sore as it would have been, had I not worked at the plantation. Tomorrow will be the big day for this project. Austin has agreed to help. I'll have him down below, cutting the sheets of plywood that will need custom fitting. I will also hire a day laborer. I had seen an index card on the bulletin board at the lumber yard offering such services. The eight-foot sheets of plywood will be awkward to handle by myself, and having a helper should assure the completion of that portion of this job.

I make the call to the lumber yard in the morning and ask if they can get the number off their bulletin board. I call the laborer. He's free to help and will be out within the hour. He arrives in an old, beat-up Oldsmobile. He's a young black man with a muscular build, which is what I need more than any particular skill. He tells me his name is Sam. I shake his hand, introduce him to Austin, then we ascend to the roof. The old wood comes off fast. Tipi is freaking out with all the noise, but I'm afraid that he'd get struck by falling debris if I let him out. I engage Sam in small talk, and he tells me that he was going to play safety for Virginia Commonwealth, but he tore his Achilles tendon playing tennis. He is proving to be a hard worker and I bet he would've been a good football player.

Now all the old wood has been torn off and we're ready to put the plywood up. It seems strange to see inside the cottage from the roof, and once again I'm glad that the weather cooperated. We take twenty minutes for lunch and then get back to task. Austin runs a power cord outside and sets up his saw horses. Soon we're in full production. Sam is good with a hammer, much better than me, and I think I'll give him a dollar an hour more than what he's asked for. We get the plywood on in good time and he says that we could get the ice-and-water shield on before nightfall as well. I tell him that I thought I could save that for another day, but he says that it would be an awkward job to do by myself, not to mention that I wouldn't have to worry about rain anymore. I really don't want to work till night-fall, but his reasoning is good and I agree to it. Austin's services are no longer needed, but he makes us each a sandwich, then heads back to his cottage with Tipi trailing behind him.

By seven o'clock our goal is met. I'm tired and sore, but the good feeling of having this task completed trumps my physical depletion. I pay Sam and thank him for the hard work, giving him the enhanced wage, and he thanks me as well. Then I clean up, unwind for a bit, and retire early.

I begin shingling the next morning. It will be a two day job, but there's still no rain in the forecast so I don't feel rushed. Austin comes over around noon to fix a lunch, but instead, I talk him into going into North Shores with me and eating at the diner. We arrive at the peak of their lunch rush and have to wait for a table. I look around and spot Molly, who is scurrying from her table to the kitchen. I feel awkward eyeing her with Austin at my side; after all, he was Renee's father. I wonder what he would hope for, if he knew that I had feelings for Molly. I try to imagine what he would do, had he been put in such a situation. I have always pictured him as a salt-of-the-earth type fellow, someone whom I felt made sound decisions with consistency. As I contemplate, he taps my shoulder and points to an open table. As we check the menu, I wonder if how Molly will react when she sees me, and how I'll react as well. I suddenly feel clumsy, like I'm thinking too hard about how to posture myself. I divert my focus. "What are you having?" I ask Austin.

He stares a little longer at the menu, then lowers it and says, "That hot turkey sandwich with mashed potatoes and gravy sounds pretty good."

I find it on the menu. It does sound good, and I've been so preoccupied that I haven't thought of what I wanted. "I think I'll get one, too," I say.

The waitress I had the other day comes and takes our order. She recognizes me and mentions that Molly is working. I tell her that I've spotted her, too, but thank her just the same. I wish that she wouldn't have mentioned it in front of Austin—now I feel uncomfortable on two fronts. But the old man doesn't react, and I choose not to delve into the matter today.

Minutes later I feel a hand on my shoulder. It's Molly. "Hey there," she says in a measured tone. "Just wanted to stop by and say hello, but I'm slammed right now so I can't talk. But it's good to see you again."

Like a dumb ass I don't say anything. I only nod and smile. I wish that my first contact with her would have been under different circumstances. For all the times I came here alone and it was slow, it had to be quite the opposite today. Furthermore, I didn't perceive any reaction from her. I want to know what kind of impact my sudden departure had on her and what she thinks of me now. For now I have to be content that she didn't shun me.

After eating at the diner, I find it hard to motivate myself to work on the roof. My first encounter with Molly since Labor Day was less than I had hoped for and leaves me with unanswered questions. Also, until this afternoon, I hadn't considered Austin's feelings concerning me dating again and I feel I have to talk to him about it. Yet, Sam's work ethic from the day before was a good influence on me and I force myself to stick with the job.

The next day is much the same, minus the trip to the diner. I want to have a day between visits so I don't seem desperate. Plus, this project isn't an enjoyable one and I want to be done with it. Then finally, around six-thirty, I finish. I climb down the ladder and walk backwards until I can view the whole roof. It looks good and I feel pride in my accomplishment.

With the roof completed and the urgency of my other tasks

less critical, I take a more leisurely pace and simply enjoy being at the cottage. Again I notice how quickly time passes when I'm out here. By mid May I begin taking an afternoon swim. In the evenings I walk the shoreline with Tipi, then listen to the Oriole game with Austin. But my breakfasts belong to Molly and the North Shores Diner.

I had a chance to talk with her shortly after I'd went to the diner with Austin. That visit reassured me that good things were still possible. She listened as I gave my synopsis, which amounted to a sales pitch, I guess, and she was not only understanding, but she went as far as to say that my actions showed how much I loved my wife and children and I should never be embarrassed by that period in my life. I asked her if she would like to do something again, and she said that she would. I told her that I wanted to speak with Austin first—to get his blessing. She understood this also. That was over a month ago now and I still haven't spoken with him about the matter. This morning at breakfast I sense that Molly's getting impatient with me as she's being shorter than usual, and I decide it's time to have that conversation with my father-in-law.

I call her and ask if she wants to go have a picnic at the state park, which is a mere five miles north of my cottage, on a small peninsula that juts out into the Atlantic. For as close as it is, I haven't been there since Mom and Dad had taken Julia and me some thirty years ago. Molly says that she'd like to go, and I say that I'll pick her up at three. I pat my leg and summon Tipi and we head down the path toward Austin's. I notice how the grass is beaten down and how the path is clear and obvious. When we were young and would only be here for a few weeks out of the summer the path was less defined. I always had to look for where it began. Now, with Austin and I using it numerous times each day it is quite distinct.

I feel unexpectedly self-confident as I approach Austin's

cottage. I believe that surviving the brutality of the streets puts tasks like this one into perspective. Yet, I want to be sensitive to his feelings. During the month that I waited to have this conversation I did a lot of soul searching. And with that I concluded that neither the memory of Renee and the children nor myself would be scarred in any way by me seeing Molly. I went on to think that I could even make love with another woman if the situation was right, as that love would be separate and distinct, and most importantly, lesser than, the love I had with Renee. The only rider I have is that I will never again marry.

I knock on the front door but don't get an answer. I try to look inside, but with the sun shining on the screen I can't see anything. Finally I hear, "Come in, Carl," and Tipi and I go inside. "Have a seat," he says, pointing toward the kitchen table and not the couch that I was heading to. "I made an apple pie and it's still warm." Without asking if I want any, he cuts me a slice, puts it on a saucer and puts a scoop of ice cream on top.

I hesitantly sit at the table. I want to delve into the topic I came here to discuss, but I practice patience and cut a fork full of pie. He comes to the table and places a plate in front of him. He looks at me and smiles as if he's going to speak, then focuses on the slice of pie in front of him. I know that timing is significant, so I wait until we finish eating before I speak. "That sure was good," are my first words, to which he wholeheartedly agrees. "But there's something important to me that I need to discuss with you," I say.

His smile disappears and is replaced by a look of worry, which I suppose is understandable considering my more recent past. I readjust my chair so I face him, rest my elbows on the table and clasp my hands together. I don't know how to begin, so I just do. "This is going to be a difficult topic for me, Austin, as I don't even know how I feel about it myself. How would it affect you if I were to go out socially with another woman?"

A smile comes back to his face, but it's a softer smile, a smile of acceptance. "Carl, you do it," he says, and he pauses for a long while before adding. "I know how much you loved my daughter, and I believe no one can ever keep her from being number one in your heart for all eternity. Enough time has passed and you're too young to spend the rest of your life alone." He rises and picks his plate off the table and pats me on the back, then turns and brings the plate to the sink.

I stand to leave and he turns to me. "I know that was a hard thing to bring up, Carl, and I appreciate the fact that you still value my opinion."

"You'll always be my father-in-law," I say, and then I nod, summon Tipi, and we walk back down the grassy path with the ocean breeze seemingly blowing in a new era for me.

Tipi runs into the cottage and I close the screen door behind him. "Sorry boy. I've gotta run to town," I say apologetically. I stop at the five-and-dime store first. There's a picnic basket in the storage shed, but it hasn't been used in many years and I assume that it's either beyond recoverability or not worth the effort. I leave the five-and-dime with a new basket. I stop at the deli and have them make several sandwiches and I pick up some hard rolls.

I'm just leaving the outer end of town when I see smoke coming out of a house. I slow down, then pull over to the side of the road. It's far enough on the outskirts where there are no other houses in sight. It looks serious, and I pelt myself with questions: is anyone in the house, is the fire department on their way and have they even been notified, or am I the only one who knows that this house is ablaze. I tell myself to go back to the cottage—that someone else will see the flames be-fore too long, but I can't get myself to drive away. Nor can I get myself to go into the house and see if anyone's inside, even though it's becoming increasingly obvious that it's what I have to do. Finally, I haul out of the car and slam the door, swearing, "Shit!" as I head for the building.

As I approach I look up to the second floor where the smoke is coming from. I balk for another moment, then force myself to do what I know I must. I open the door and yell, "Is anyone in here?" I don't hear anything and I go back outside and look up and down the street, hoping to hear sirens or see an emergency vehicle approaching. But there isn't any and I stand on the porch for a moment, nervously running my hand through my hair, not wanting to enter again, but not seeing another option that I could employ quickly enough to save the lives of anyone who might be inside. "Fuck!" I cry, and I open the door and rush inside.

I run from room to room throughout the downstairs and see no one. I go to the stairway that leads to the upstairs and cautiously climb four or five steps. I hear the fury of the fire—the sound of crackling wood and the roar that flames make when a fire has reached an intense level. I smell the smoke and see it cascade across the hardwood floor from my right to my left. I climb one more step, then after pausing, climb another. I'm fighting myself. I don't want to go any farther. I yell out again. No answer. I feel the heat now and tell myself that nobody could be alive if they were up there. I turn to leave, but get a mental image of a child huddled in a corner, or a baby in a crib choking on the smoke. Having lost my own children, I take a deep breath and think no more and run up the final seven steps and into the hall. There are three doors, one of them is open and the other two are closed. I run into the open room and look around. There are no flames in this room but the heat from the next room is causing the walls to smoke and they'll burst into flames soon. I rip the covers off the bed, look in the closet and then behind the door but I see no one, so I run out of the room, halfway down the stairs and draw a deep breath. I'm committed now—no longer questioning whether I should or shouldn't do this. I fill my lungs again and fly back up the stairs and to the closer of the two rooms with closed doors. The doorknob is hot and I singe my hand as I turn it open. The heat throws me back as I enter and it's brutality makes me shorten my search to a yell and a quick scan of the room before running for the stairwell again.

I know the last room will be the worst. I was hoping to find someone in one of the other rooms who would tell me that they were the only one in the house, but with that not occurring I have to go in. I look downstairs, still hoping to see a fireman burst through the door, yelling for me to come down and saying that he'll get it from here, but that's not happening either. I suck down a deep breath and head in again. This time the knob is too hot to grab and I have to kick the door in, and when I do I'm knocked over by the heat. I shoot back to my feet and move sideways to the door, the way one would when adding wood to a blazing bonfire, then turn my face forward long enough to yell if anyone is in the room. I see movement in the corner. Without thinking, I dash through the flames and over to the area where I had seen motion. There's nobody there. It was an optical illusion from looking through the heated air.

I know now that nobody is in the house and I can get the hell out with a clear conscience. However I'm choking and I know I have to move quickly. I shield my face with my arm and make a dash, but as I rush through the center of the room I trip on a beam that had fallen and hit my head on the side of the bed, momentarily stunning myself. I feel my leg being scorched and I crawl ahead and away from the flames. Out of breath, I gasp for air, taking in a lung full of smoke. I'm dizzy from the fall, but, from my knees, I lunge forward again. I'm choking badly and the smoke at floor level is thick and it has disoriented me and already I feel a strange lightheadedness. I'm out of air and I can't draw a decent breath. I push myself up to my knees again, knowing that I have to get out immediately, but this time I can only manage to topple forward. Glancing behind me, I see that my right pant leg is on fire, and I know I'm in trouble because I can't feel any pain. I want to flop down and succumb to this—to just give up—but instinct makes me drive on and I pull myself toward the stairwell. I think of everything I've been through and how I'm just now beginning to regain my life. I'm within five feet of the door when more of the ceiling collapses and lands upon me with a thunderous, fiery burst. I'm too weary to fight anymore. And nobody was in the house! *I can't believe I'm going to die in vain!* is my last thought.

CHAPTER THIRTEEN

The streets are dirty and unrecognizable as I walk through an unknown town. I have no clue as to why I'm here or how I got here and I feel as strange as these surroundings. The buildings I pass seem modern and lavish at first, but upon closer look there's something wrong with them—something that I can't quite account for or explain, and there's deterioration with each moment that passes. The people walking by are casual and have quasi-sophisticated airs. They don't appear to be happy or sad, but with that, don't appear to be void of emotion either. Yet, even though they're not exuberant, they seem methodical, self-reliant, and centered. Nobody seems to be in a hurry to get anywhere, nor do they seem like they have time to waste. I recognize no one but I find them very curious, but again, there is something mysteriously lacking in them, and like in the edifices I pass, it's something that I can't define.

I come to a park that's in the center of the town. There's a river flowing through, banked by well-trimmed fertile green grasses that flow into a slope that leads down to the waters. People are sitting on both sides of the bank, chatting and laughing with each other. They're dressed in the attire of the roaring twenties and I notice a rich mixture of nationalities amongst them. There are no ugly people, nor any that are striking. I'm drawn to the pleasantness of the scene and find an unoccupied spot and sit. I feel rather comfortable and come to think that I'll be all right here, wherever this place may be. There are boulders in the river that the waters splash against, and some of the spray cools my face, though the bright sunshiny day already provides a near perfect temperature. I feel somewhat good for the first time since I arrived as I watch the river flow, but my perception subtly changes, just as it had with the buildings downtown, as I notice a dead fish snagged in a bundle of sticks that have wedged between two of the rocks. I observe too that there's a rusted-out pail on the bank across from me, as well as a bunch of beer cans. The more I look, I see that the whole bank is littered with trash and the ground next to where I'm sitting is dotted with various wrappers, used prophylactics, dog feces, discarded tampons; and I can't believe that I had ever found this place to be serene. I get up feeling blasé and confused. Walking back toward the street I see that the grass is dry and yellow, and the skies that were so blue a moment ago have the same yellowish hue as the grass. I get up and abandon this once-quixotic utopia, now deeply concerned about my well being and future.

Nothing is making any sense to me. I meditate as I walk, trying to determine what took me from point A to point B, but although I can sense that I have that knowledge inside me, there's a barrier which I can't get beyond. I look at the names of the streets, the signs on buildings and the names of businesses, searching for clues as to where I am. I wave at a elderly woman who's approaching me and she stops, but when I try to question her, I can't speak. I look for climatic references. The trees are deciduous, but that could place me most anywhere. It would've left me more of a clue had they been predominantly tropical or coniferous. I finally abandon the effort, but not the contemplation.

I feel to be on the verge of panic—not the running down the streets with arms flailing panic, but the inner panic that can be the most tormenting. I realize I need to step aside and collect myself, a lesson I've learned from my time on the streets. There's a stone ledge protruding from the foundation of a building and I climb upon it and sit. I close my eyes and try to blot out everything that surrounds me. I want to see Austin. He's always had a calming influence upon me, with the exception of the eighteen month anniversary of the tragedy that we shared. I picture him and imagine what he'd say to me now. *Just go where the path takes you, Carl. Everything happens for a reason,* is what I picture him saying. I feel somewhat better, but panic returns when I again open my eyes. I concentrate. I had found solace seconds earlier, so, whether it was sage advice or simply bullshit manufactured by random brain waves, I abide by what I had thought and follow the road.

I come to a bridge that crosses a slow flowing river. Directly beyond that the road splits into three. Without conscious effort, my thinking turns into a symbolic analysis as I try to choose which tributary to take. The scenery on the first street looks the same as what I've been experiencing since I got here and I eliminate it from consideration. The second one looks strikingly similar to one from the town where I was born. The third has an Asian flavor to it, with colorful, character-scripted neon signs and open-air markets. I choose the middle street and proceed.

I walk to the end of the first block and see that I'm at the intersection of Oak and Fourth—I grew up on the intersection of Oak Ridge and Fifteenth. I look down the next block and see that it's a residential area. The houses look familiar to the ones that were in our neighborhood, but none of them are exact matches. I search for a meaning as I continue to walk. When

I get to the end of the block, on the corner of Oak and Fifth, I see the house that I have now anticipated seeing. I go up the familiar walkway, up the four cement steps and onto the front porch. There's a sign on the door that says OPEN HOUSE. I turn the doorknob and enter. The flight of stairs directly in front of where I stand curves to the right as it ascends, instead of to the left. I climb the eighteen stairs; that much is the same. There's only one open door and I enter that room. In it there's a child's bed, a dresser, a nightstand with a small lamp, and a hamper. On the wall is a pennant that says *WASHINGTON SENATORS*. If I were in a different state of being I'd surely have a chill go through me. Now, I'm simply immersed in nostalgia. I take a moment and drink in this atmosphere, then go back to the streets, which are now a comfortable place for me to search for truth.

The next day begins in much the same way, even though I don't recall having slept or that it got dark or anything that would denote a change of days; still, for the purpose of differentiation, I refer to it as the next day. I'm again walking down the street, the same one I'd traversed the day before. From a distance, amongst the unfamiliar faces, I see someone I recognize. I squint to get a better focus, checking to see if perhaps my eyes were playing tricks on me, then see that indeed I know this person, although I can't recall his name. He went to the same high school as me but I don't know much about him, except that he was quiet and ordinary. As I get within earshot he calls my name. I look at his face; the lower half of his chin is missing and the flesh is exposed but he isn't bleeding. "What the hell happened to you?" I ask, dreading whatever the answer might be. "Oh, just a little car wreck," he says. "Looks like a fire got the best of you, Morgan." I look down and see that the lower part of my pants have been burned off and that my legs are badly scorched. I look at my arms, my chest and stomach. Horrified, I leave the man and run to the slow-moving river and look at my reflection in a small pool that forms at the footings of the bridge. I see the grotesque scar of melted skin on my cheeks, neck and forehead. I recall the fire and I wonder what had happened to me, and the questions of where am I and how did I get here are replaced by *Why am I here?* I have flashbacks of my absentminded drive to Pennsylvania and the subsequent sojourn to D.C. and I wonder if, again, I've fallen into that same state of mind.

I feel the need to find someone I know, not some forgotten classmate from high school, but someone that was a part of my everyday life. I run back to the streets and venture into the heart of the city, farther into this town than I've yet gone. I see birds perched on a power line; many of their feathers are missing, making them look patchy and unhealthy. In the alley is a three-legged cat. He looks at me and hisses, but gets behind me and follows my path. I glance behind and he stops and looks at me with a judgmental glare. "Go away!" I yell, and he shuts one eye, which makes it appear that he's taunting me with a wink. He sits on the sidewalk and waits for me to continue. I give up and try to ignore him as I continue my search, but occasionally stop and look back, only to see that he matches my pace and stops when I stop. He winks at me again. "This is fucked-up!" I yell. "Get the fuck away from me!" But the cat is unfettered.

I become resigned to the fact that the cat will follow me, but as I do this, he is no longer around. I continue my search for a familiar face. I think about my earlier encounter and how my classmate pointed out my wounds. I look down at my legs again an glance at my reflection in a window. I see a bench, go to it and sit, and realize the need to come to understand where I am. I figure three things are possible: first, I have slipped back into a state of dementia; second, someone slipped me a hallucinogen; or third, I died in the fire. It's the latter possibility that intrigues me most. Yet, the possibility of that event having happened, which I now believe to be true, depends on the invalidity of the first two possibilities. But the deceptive nature of each of those two eliminates any chance of certainty. I dissect them one by one, beginning with dementia. When I was on the streets of D.C. I realized that I was fucked up, and I don't really feel that way now. Furthermore, just hours before the fire I was interacting with people at the diner, something I wouldn't have done in a maddened state. Also, I did feel clear-headed when I pulled up to the burning house. I realize that the second possibility would make a the illusion of a burning house seem real and would explain the quasi-psychedelic characteristics of the place I'm in now, but there wasn't anyone whom I associated with in North Shores that would have slipped me anything. Besides, the burning house was just a fire. There were no talking flames, no walls with arms of fire reaching out for me. Everything in the fire occurred quite the way it was supposed to. I lower my head with the realization of the final option. I am dead!

The next step is to go back to the question, *Where am I?* I think of the religion of my upbringing and recall no polluted rivers or winking cats. Yet, it seems that I've entered some sort of afterlife existence, be it a form of the purgatory I was told about or the disembodied state experienced by the ghosts of lore. Either way, I feel no sense of love. Nor do I feel the presence of God. Nonetheless, I sense that there's something to be accomplished here, although I'm not yet sure what that is.

I get up and begin to walk, hoping to find something that will help make sense of this situation.

CHAPTER FOURTEEN

I enter the third segment of this existence that I'm in. I decide to call it a segment because, as I said before, there are no days or nights here, even though there are periods that resemble both, but they come at non-concentric times. I've now come to accept the fact that my earthly existence has ended, but I've yet to meet Jesus or Buddha or anyone else of the like. I'm just isolated in an inexplicable nether-where. Still, the belief I had of the afterlife when I was on earth seems to have been substantiated. I had always questioned scientific explanations of life's origin and the origin of the cosmos. The Big Bang theory always left me questioning how matter could create itself and where the catalytic speck of dust came from. Now I feel as though I'm about to find that out, along with every question I had ever had.

A unique element in this segment is that I'm able to see the happenings of the world that I left behind. I look upon my Virginia home and see Julia's husband helping sort through my belongings. He's evaluating a keepsake of mine, something with great sentimental value to me and something that I'd been careful with and cherished from my youth through my adulthood and until the day I died, and upon slight consideration, he takes it and throws it into a box that's designated for the trash. Julia is introspective as she looks through photos, and thinks of how sad it is that I met my demise just when I seemed to be on the verge of putting some semblance of life back together. She cries soundlessly and turns her head so Jim can not see. He is still going through boxes of my memorabilia, throwing most of it away but keeping a few things to make it seem like he's putting effort into it. He's getting frustrated and antsy, but in his head he's been calculating how much profit he'll make off the sale of my house. He recalls that he used to be afraid of me and how guarded he had to be when I was around, hoping I'd never get wind that he'd slap Julia around whenever he got drunk. He thinks of what a relief it was when I went off the deep end and became a harmless dove, and what more of a relief it is now that I'm dead.

Julia gets up and walks out of the room. She tells Jim that she's going out for air when he asks, but she's reminiscing over our youth and doesn't want to be interrupted by his negativity. She begins walking down the sidewalk. Passing a playground, she thinks of how safe she would feel whenever I'd walk with her when we went to school, and with that, the cry she's been suppressing coughs out of her like a spasm and she clutches the fence and gasps out shameless sobs.

The children are downstairs, halfheartedly playing a video game. They are somber and miss their Uncle Carl. They were too young to remember Renee and the kids; the only reference they have to them is the occasional talk of the accident. Also, they're too young to appreciate the mental collapse I had, even though they'd seen the concern for me that their mother had shown. So to them I was nothing but ordinary. Out of all the people who knew me at the time of my death, this was a view that only they held.

In the place I'm in, I look at everything I see strictly as

knowledge. I feel the love Julia feels for me, but I don't, or rather can not, feel any sorrow for her grief, nor do I have feelings of anger toward Jim. I only see it in a factual manner, something that I can't alter or influence. From there my thoughts go to Austin. He's sitting at the kitchen table at his cottage playing solitaire, as he usually does in the afternoon. In the corner of the room lies Tipi, snuggled upon a rug, his eyes half-open and staring into a nothingness that seems to represent the day. Austin's suit, the one he wore to my funeral, is still in the living room, the coat folded in half and resting atop the pants that are draped across an arm of the sofa. He is in a solemn mood. Although he misses my company, he's feeling guilty for thinking that my death may have been the best thing that could have happened to me. He felt that, despite my ultimate recollection of everything and the positive path it put me on, I would never achieve full respectability with anyone who didn't know and love me prior to losing my faculties. But despite his perception of other people's perceptions, he cared about me and continued to think of me as a son-in-law even after Renee died.

Following in the overtones of Austin's thoughts, I think of the people whom I lived with on the streets. Of course, Don comes to mind first and I find him living in small-town Arkansas, in a small apartment similar in scale to the shack we had lived in. After Florida, he decided to give the real world a try again, and like me, the plantation was the necessary step for him to make the transition to normalcy. But he never took the chance of trying for legal assimilation. He chose to work at a hardware store for cash, getting paid under the table in return for anonymity. He doesn't know of my death and he never will hear of it while in his earthly existence, but he does think of me on occasion and hopes that things have worked out for me. He longs to get back to the west coast, but, even though he doesn't yet know it, he has lung cancer and will never return to his home.

I look in on the others. They are still on the streets, although Joe has gone from Washington to Baltimore. They'll all spend the rest of their days there, eventually dying on them, with the exception of Gene, who'll live long enough to be put in a senior care facility, and Banana, who'll be killed by a county jail inmate when he's incarcerated for indecent exposure.

Finally, I view how my death is being taken at the North Shores Diner. The summation of the scuttlebutt would be the crazy man who died trying to do a good deed—a recap that, although not entirely flattering, is probably fair. I see that some of the patrons that I had talked to over the past couple years had actually been pulling for me, while to others I was more of an annoyance; someone whom they felt obliged to return the engagement of conversation for the sake of fulfilling their humanitarian commitment. Nothing that I didn't perceive while I was alive.

Molly is on a break. This day has been hard on her and she's standing outside the back door having a cigarette, something she hasn't done in over four years. Besides the grief she feels over my death, and the contemplation of the void she'll have in her life, she worries about her future. She considers herself homely and sees the aging process accelerating rapidly. With this, she wonders what the future holds for her. Inwardly, she had hoped that our relationship would evolve to the point where I'd ask her to marry me. Now, she wonders if she'll be alone for the remainder of her days. Sadly, I know that she will.

CHAPTER FIFTEEN

I rise from a deep and tranquil sleep. It's the first time I've slept since I've entered this existence and I rise feeling refreshed and renewed. I scan my environs and perceive a change in everything that surrounds me. The streets that had seemed so lifeless, despite the pedestrian traffic, are now brimming and vital. The people that mill about wear smiles and for the first time they talk freely amongst each other. I look at the park and it, too, appears different. The river and the field are once again green and free from litter and the pleasant smell of newly-mown grass stirs my senses. The air is warm and the breeze is gentle. And I feel something different about myself as well; an inner resurgence and an understanding that there's a purpose for being here. I comprehend that this is a state of passage, not a final destination, and that I have to be receptive to the reason that I'm here.

I thirst for contact, so I head toward the business district. I begin greeting the people on the streets, the ones whom I had thought to be serving a purposeless existence. Now they're friendly and interactive and I sense substance in all of them. "Good morning," I say to a young woman with radiant skin and flowing black hair. "How are you?"

"Hello Carl," she replies cheerfully. "See, it wasn't so bad, now was it?"

I feel no shock that she knows my name, even though I've never seen her before. I reply to her, "No, it wasn't that bad at all, although I was concerned and disoriented at first."

"We all felt that at first, Carl. But you're not quite through yet. Go downtown and look around."

I look down the street and then back toward her, but she's already merged into the crowd. I proceed and am drawn to the third building on the right hand side. The sign on the window says **Department of Information.** I enter and browse around. There is a display of books on a stand in the middle of the main aisle. I pick them up one by one and look at the titles. I see, *It Wasn't Your Fault,* and *Nothing Has Changed—We're Still Here,* and *No One is Better Than You.* I begin to memorize the titles for later contemplation, but then I see a sign that says that the books are free. I take one of each, then head for the tranquillity of the riverbank.

I take a spot where a slow ripple in the stream sends forth soothing sounds. There's a woman next to me who appears to be Indian or Pakistani. I nod and smile.

"You look nice today, Carl," she says. She points to my legs first, then to my abdomen and then to my face.

I look down and seen that the hideous scars of charred flesh are no longer on my legs. I get up and scamper down to the water and see that my face has been restored as well. I turn to the woman with a wondrous look, and she stands, waves, then walks away. I sit back down and pick up the books and meditate on their titles. I feel like I have an opportunity to transcend this place, but that something has to be achieved here before I can move on. I hold the first book in my hands. *It Wasn't Your Fault,* I think as I contemplate the title. I think about the accident and my reaction to the news of Renee and the children's deaths. "It wasn't my fault," I say aloud. I close my eyes and scenes begin flashing through my mind, subliminal thoughts that I'd had on Earth but I never allowed myself to recognize. I envision myself walking down the streets of Fredericksburg and ignoring a person who passed along a kind word, and then thinking, *That was the father of one of Daniel's friends. He probably thinks you're a goof. Daniel's memory deserves better!* I think of how it bothered me that I had done so much classroom work at home, and how if I hadn't we would have done more as a complete family, I would have been driving the night of the accident and either it would have been avoided or I would have been killed with them. I drop the book and ponder the significance of my thoughts.

I grab the second book from the grass, *Nothing Has Changed—We're Still Here.* I think of how I had questioned my belief in the afterlife. I had spent much time worrying that my beloved Renee, Daniel, and Prudence had passed in a way that was equitable to them never having existed. Based on that logic, I wondered what good a memory could be if it passed when I passed. The depression I had felt over that was specifically what sent me into my personal oblivion. Now in this post-metabolic existence I realize that my loved ones still are what they always were.

I take the final book and contemplate the title, *No One is Better Than You.* Again I close my eyes as I think. Here, my thoughts go primarily to the streets of Washington D.C. I remember the people who frowned upon me and despised the very sight of me. Moreover, I recall how I had come to accept their view—that I was a lesser-than in the great opinion bank of humanity. I came to accept the view that there comes a time for all of us when we were more than we are and that that time had simply come early for me. I think of the guilt I felt for ill-serving the memory of my family by allowing myself to be that way. I see now that what I experienced was unavoidable, based upon who I was and the things that I had experienced upon my life's path. With that absolution, I again drift off into a rest.

When I wake up I see that the sunny day has yielded to a thick, hanging fog. I rise and walk away from the river and to the middle of the field. From out of the fog I see three shadowy figures. It's the same scene as I had in the dream; the first dream I had of Renee and the kids when I was on the streets of Washington. This time, however, they are closer than before and they emerge from the fog. The look of love on Renee's face is too pure to be described by the most splendid poet. It's the look she wore after we had made love on a stormy summer night, while public radio played a Chopin waltz in the background. She stands next to me now and I feel one with her, and the love radiates so that I have no need to embrace or kiss or make love to her. Everything I sense she perceives, and we share the experience of unblemished love.

Daniel comes to me next. Through his thoughts I know that all is right. I know that the humility I experienced in my last two years was not a source of shame for him, but something that was natural, uncompromising, unavoidable, and something to be totally understood. I touch him, putting my hand on his shoulder, and a warmth comes over me. He is still my child, yet now he is also my equal, and I relate to him on both levels.

My reunion is complete when Prudence comes to me. She is radiant like an angel and as beautiful as anything I have ever seen. I reach out and touch her cheek, drawing my fingers down her soft skin. She has been waiting for me to arrive, and she is complete now that I'm here. She forgives me for feeling guilty about what the earth had deprived her of, and now that I'm here I understand that it hadn't deprived her of anything. I take the three of them and hold them in an embrace. Then

Renee speaks. "Others are waiting for you, too," she says, and she smiles. She takes my hand, turns, and we follow, and the whiteness we had been standing in turns into an earthy path bordered by green grass and glorious flowers with a blue sky, white clouds and bright yellow sun.